A Nacho

Patio Ca

Who Plugged the Dyke?

For Jill –
You should have
a complete set.

By Steve Schatz

Ordering Information:

Quantity sales. Special discounts are available on quantity purchases by corporations, associations, and others. For details, contact the publisher at the address above.

Orders by U.S. trade bookstores and wholesalers. Please contact Ingram.

Available in Print, Audio, & Ebook

Published by Any Summer Sunday Books
AnySummerSundayCom, LLC
520 S. Walnut #3306, Bloomington, IN 47404
Info@AnySummerSunday.com

ISBN: 978-1-953029-02-7 PRINT
978-1-953029-99-7 EBOOK
978-1-953029-05-8 AUDIO

A Nacho Mama's
Patio Café Novel

Who Plugged the Dyke?

By Steve Schatz

Any Summer Sunday Books ◄▲▼▲► Bloomington, IN

Other Books by Steve Schatz

From Absolute Love Publishing

- Adima Rising
- Adima Returning

From Any Summer Sunday Books

- Any Summer Sunday at Nacho Mama's Patio Café
- Ghost Girl | A Mystery

It's Fiction

This is a work of fiction. All characters, places and situations are the invention of the author. All names and places are used fictitiously. Any similarities between this work and any other realities in any dimensions or timelines are completely coincidental.

Please: If you enjoy this book, tell your friends and post a review on your favorite book sites.

ACKNOWLEDGMENTS

Thanks to those brave few who attacked beta versions of the book – Theresa Atkinson, Debra Walsh, Wednesday Sorokin, and Pat Vint. Rox for the bosom of the sisterhood. The little Dutch boy who went there first. Elizabeth Cure for initial inspiration (through no fault of her own). Erica Berent for the Any Summer Sunday logo. Wednesday Sorokin and Sharon Bruno for cover inspiration (which I then mangled). James from GoOnWrite.com for final cover design. Michael Mullen for permission to use his wonderful songs and for on-going genius.

DEDICATION

As always – to my beloved ... who endures this weird old man with remarkable grace.

Chapter One
The Bomb

Stepping out of the dark bar, the late afternoon sun blinded me. Squinting, I scanned for Deb. Shouldn't be too hard. How many 5'10", 230-pound lesbians adorned in judge's robes, a cowboy hat, and black combat boots could be roaming the streets of our little college town on a Sunday afternoon? As my eyes adjusted to the glare, I spotted her. She was heading toward her beloved Boomer, a rust-colored pickup truck of mixed heritage that fairly screamed, 'Come on down, gals . . . a free checkered shirt with every ride!' I had ridden in Boomer before and waves of testosterone coursed through my body just by sitting in the thing.

Deb was hiking up her robe, digging for her keys in some nether region I prayed would forever remain a mystery, exposing black fishnet stockings and the edge of the dominatrix leather mini she wore to her rally at the bar. The look went over well inside *Hoosier Daddy*, the town's only gay bar. However, her next event was at the *Magawatta Ladies' Garden and Debate Society*, a more upscale and tightly wound crowd. I had never dreamed she would be allowed to speak before that group, much less be invited by the current president, Judge '*I am Always Right so Sit Down or Else*' Walker. I hoped she planned to keep her robes securely fastened. The invite was just one more delightful surprise in a two- week period that kept ladling lucky breaks all over Deb. Unless something very bad happened to her very soon and very publicly, it looked like Deborah Eubank was going to be the very first wide open, in your face, no excuses, if you have a problem with it, that's *your* problem, lesbian to be elected to be a judge in the very red state of Indiana.

Unfortunately, I had a problem. Deb's briefcase was in my hand and she was much closer to Boomer than to me. She was going to reach the truck first and once she started that super calibrated, jacked-up noise machine—bedecked with a myriad of shiny things that whistled, bellowed, and spun—there was no way she would be able to hear me calling.

I sighed. This was going to require running and yelling, two things I actively avoid as individual acts and absolutely refuse to do at the same time. But I was the campaign manager and I was paid to do three things—keep track of her schedule, babysit her beloved chihuahua Slasher, and make sure Deb always had her briefcase.

The day's schedule was complete. She was on her way to the final event of the day. Slasher was happily ensconced in the bar's courtyard café, enjoying tidbits offered by Beau and Aunt May at our regular table and would be picked up later. But Deb had forgotten her briefcase . . . again. And although *she* was the one who left it, *I* was the one who would be blamed and subjected to a *glare de dyke,* which would hurt longer than rallying my less than toned body for a brief jog.

So, despite inner voices screaming in horror and hurling accusations of abuse, I began to run toward her at top speed. Unfortunately, as I am regularly successful in ignoring all exhortations to exercise, my top speed was not the graceful glide of a cheetah I saw in my mind. Roger, observing one of the few times I was forced to run, claimed I resembled a three-legged hippo attempting to walk a tightrope during an earthquake. He was being unnecessarily catty in my opinion.

However, it became quickly clear that Deb was closing the gap to Boomer faster than I was closing the gap to Deb. Running was not enough and failure promised more pain and embarrassment than the alternative, horrifying as it was. There are times that a poof's gotta do what a poof's gotta do. I raised my voice to Miss Thing tenor and volume. "Deb!" I called. "Woo hoo. Deb!" If any onlookers held questions about the quantity and quality of my manliness after seeing me run, the high-pitched call left no doubt. I waved the briefcase over my head, continuing to shout and run.

Black spots swam before my eyes and my brain reeled from lack of oxygen. My body screamed that such mistreatment would not go unpunished for days to come. I wasn't going to last long, but Saint Lance, the patron saint of middle-aged homos, smiled down at my efforts and tapped Deb on the shoulder. She turned, having finally fished out her keys, saw me, and took a few steps in my direction as I whimpered to a stop, holding out the briefcase, too winded to breathe.

She grabbed it. "Oh, thanks, BB. I don't know why I keep leaving it." She looked at me with concern. "Are you okay?"

Gasping, I nodded. She smiled. "Take the rest of the day off. I'll handle the *Debate Society* and pick up Slasher on the way home. You look a bit weary." She squeezed my shoulder, then hit the button on her key ring to unlock Boomer's doors.

The explosion seemed to unfold in slow motion. I had a great view over Deb's shoulder. First the cab of the truck filled with flame. Then a roaring boom shattered the windshield. The doors flew open, but somehow, stayed attached. A rolling wave of heat hit me about the same time that a flying Deb did the same thing. The heat, though intense, I could have handled. However, Deb, who no one would call petite, leveled me. Had she not turned moments before to take her briefcase, I would probably have been awash in pieces of Deb. As it was, I got the whole enchilada – 230 muscular pounds flying through the air, bringing me to the ground in a position I had never intended to be in with a woman. I think I broke her fall. I'm not sure what she broke, but I wasn't going to be walking right for a while. Pinned beneath her, face to face, both of us breathless and shocked, it took a moment to get our bearings.

A look of concern crossed Deb's face. "Are you okay?"

Gasping from the combination of shock and the weight on my chest, I nodded. "You?"

Quick witted as always, Deb nodded and grinned. "We gotta stop meeting this way. If the newspapers got hold of this, they'd start vicious rumors that I'm straight."

We untangled ourselves and she helped me up. Turning to her truck, we saw it was little more than a ball of fire. "Damn it, I loved that truck. Kinda brought out my feminine side, don't you think?"

The denizens of *Hoosier Daddy* were quickly emptying onto the street to see what had happened. Nacho Mama parted the crowd like a charging rhino and grabbed us by the shoulders. "Come on, you two. This ain't an amateur job. Whoever did this is certain to be watching to make sure it worked." Looking Deb up and down, Nacho grinned. "And it's pretty obvious it didn't. I gotta get you to a safe place. So, march!"

Nacho, the proprietor of *Nacho Mama's Patio Café*, a sancto-sanctorum inside the bar, was one of those people you instinctively obeyed. A gruff restaurateur of uncertain gender, with a penchant for muumuus and cigars, Nacho ruled the patio café inside *Hoosier Daddy* with an iron hand. No one fucked with Nacho. Even Deb turned and allowed herself to be shepherded by Nacho without her usual questions and evaluations.

Sirens were screaming close now. Nacho pulled us through the crowd and into *Hoosier Daddy*. The sudden darkness blinded me as effectively as the sun had a few moments before. Nacho didn't slow, dragging us through the side door onto the now- empty patio café, heading toward the office in the back. Even in my shock, I was intrigued. I had been coming to *Hoosier Daddy* every Sunday for over five years to meet a gaggle of friends for TiaRa del Fuego's *Parade of Gowns* drag show and as far as I knew, none of us had ever made it into Nacho's inner chamber. This was definitely going to make me grand dame of the table during our tête-à-tête for the next few weeks.

Nacho pulled a ring of keys from underneath the muumuu, unlocked the door, and led us in. I experienced a bit of a letdown. It looked, well . . . like an office. I guess that's not surprising, but as we had spent many hours sipping cocktails, considering what kinds of top secret equipment and/or machines of punishment and pleasure were housed within, the final reveal was hardly worth the time invested in contemplation. I suppose if, as a kid, I had been spirited away to the North Pole and found out that Santa's workshop was really just a big factory with cement floors and lots of shelving, with all the tinsel and decorations carefully packed in boxes for shipment, the feeling would be the same.

The place was neat, very neat. One wall was filled with filing cabinets that had combination locks and external locking bars. A long desk took up another entire wall. There were several computer monitors on the desk with several computer towers underneath. It seemed to be a lot of equipment for one small restaurant, but maybe Nacho liked toys. One never knew with Nacho and we all knew better than to ask. There were several phones on the desk—not a single phone with multiple lines, but separate phones in a rainbow of colors. Nacho pushed us toward two chairs, then picked up the receiver of a lavender- colored desk phone with a single red button in the center of the face and no keypad for dialing. After listening without speaking for a few seconds, someone answered. Nacho said, "It's me. I'm on lavender. Ready? Three, two, one." Then Nacho pushed the red button, paused a moment, glared a silent order at us to be quiet, and spoke into the phone. "I have people here."

Deb and I looked at each other. She raised her eyebrow in a question. She occasionally came to *Hoosier Daddy*, but she knew that this was my hangout. She didn't know if this spy stuff was usual. My baffled expression conveyed my inability to provide any useful information. All this was new to me. It certainly was turning out to be an eventful Sunday.

Nacho continued, "It happened. Her truck. No, she's fine. No, it didn't look government, but it was professional." Nacho listened and nodded. "Yep. Start checking. I'll step up protection to level two. Later." Nacho hung up and looked at us.

"What do you mean, level two?" Deb asked. "Have you been stalking me? What's going on?"

Nacho held up a hand. "We got no time for that now."

Deb began to protest, but Nacho cut her off. "First things first " Turning to me, Nacho glared at me as only Nacho can. I'm a grown man, and I don't scare easy. However, when I came under Nacho's gaze, I'm pretty proud I didn't pee myself. "BB, are you paying attention?"

Wishing I was anywhere else, being glared at by anyone else, I responded as meekly as humanly possible, "Yes, Nacho?"

"I've known you a long time. I know you are basically a good guy. I also know you don't mind gossiping a bit here and there, especially when you're lubricated."

"Yes, Nacho." There was no reason to deny it. I enjoy dishing tea with the best and lying to Nacho was not a healthy option.

"You have already seen things that very few people have ever seen. You are going to see some more things. If you *ever* say anything about any of them to anyone, I will know. Do you believe me, BB?"

In the core of my being, I was certain. I nodded. "And if I ever do find out that you have, for any reason, let even the slightest bit of this slip, I will make you regret it, enormously, for as long as you continue to painfully gasp for air and wish for the sweet release of death. Do I make myself clear?"

I found it hard to swallow. I found it hard to breathe. I didn't want to see any more. I wanted to have all memories of what I had seen painlessly zapped away.

Perhaps Nacho could use a ray gun or a teensy electrical shock. I was definitely operating out of my depth. My comfort zone was far, far away. Everything that had happened was beyond me. All I had done was bring Deb her briefcase. The only reason I had done that was because her first campaign manager had flaked out and she needed someone to handle reporting and scheduling. She asked me and I refused. Then she offered to pay me enough that I set aside my general political disinterest and my active avoidance of anything which made me a crucial player in any high-stakes or stressful activities. My only motivation was to earn enough to buy a lovely new pair of Christian Louboutin beaded loafers which far exceeded my budget. Now I had almost been blown up and to add excitement—which I had absolutely no need of— Nacho was threatening my life.

I took a deep breath, the better not to stutter and replied, "I understand, Nacho. I won't say anything, but maybe it would be better if I left?"

“Ain't gonna happen, BB. You're needed now. But don't worry. Like I said, I've been watching you. You'll do fine, as long as you listen close and don't get killed."

Deb had recovered enough from the bomb and was not as in awe of Nacho as I. "Now wait a minute. I think it's about time we clarify some things. Nobody's going to get killed."

Nacho turned to her. "Another few feet closer to that truck and you wouldn't be here arguing. So, you’re right. *Let's clarify*. You got a good shot at making it to judge."

Deb nodded.

Nacho continued, "My sources tell me there is about to be an opening on the state supreme court and the winds are blowing in the right direction that whoever gets nominated is going to be a woman or a homo. In case you hadn’t noticed, you’re both. Plus, surprise, surprise, you are actually competent and not in anyone’s pocket. Usually that’s a bad thing, but no one can protest against your appointment because they don’t want someone else’s baby doll to get in. None of the state poobahs is all powerful at the present time, so the only play is to make sure no one else wins. That means you win by default."

Deb smiled. "I hardly think that power brokers think of potential judges as baby dolls."

Nacho snorted. "You'd be surprised. But there's more Once you are on the bench a while, if you don't screw up, you are a lesbian from a conservative state. If someone wants to make an appointment to a federal court, a dyke from a blue state ain't getting anywhere, but from a middle of the road state . . . that might actually fly. That means that federal lawsuits can be brought to your court."

"I think you're getting a bit ahead of yourself," Deb said.

"I ain't saying I'm puttin' down bets, but I have learned that keeping an eye on chess pieces is a good way to avoid certain situations. I also am aware that those who like to point to gays as the cause of everything that has ever gone wrong with the country have noticed you and this race. They have also seen the possibilities that may be comin' 'round the mountain. They know the best way to solve a problem is to keep it from ever becoming a problem."

"But this is just a county judge position," Deb protested. "It's mostly civil cases—real estate, child custody . . . things like that."

"But it can lead to other things. That's why there has been a lot of chatter about stopping you."

"So, you're saying that some right-wing conspiracy has set out to kill me?"

"No. I'm saying there has been a lot of chatter from a lot of different directions and I happen to think you'd be good for this town, plus I like your girlish figure. So, I've been keeping an eye out."

Smiling at the girlish figure crack, Deb said, "Oh, Nacho. How you talk."

"Just payin' some attention and keepin' an eye open. But this attack changes things. We've got to move into active mode. We need to get you some protection."

"No," Deb said firmly. "Nacho, I appreciate your

concern. I like your interest even more. However, I'm not going into hiding or be surrounded by bodyguards. Yes, Boomer blew up. I agree it may be a bomb, but I'm not sure it's not that new carb I installed. It might have been gas pooling."

Nacho was not used to being contradicted. Two immovable forces of nature were face to face. I took a surreptitious step backward to get out of range. Glaring, Nacho was about to respond when Deb raised her hand.

"I said no. Not without more information. I can think of four or five people off the top of my head who have the knowledge, means, and certainly the desire to do this if it does turn out to be a bomb. None are secret underground militia members. One is the father of my children. He hates me and trained as an ordinance tech in the service. A couple are jerks I twirled around my finger in court. You can look into it. I'll look into it. If we can't find answers, then we can talk about next steps. For now, I have an appearance at a party hosted by the right honorable Judge Walker. I thought hell would freeze before she endorsed me, and I will *not* be late."

Deb looked at her watch and looked at me. "I do need a ride. How 'bout it, BB?"

"What do you think about the police?" Nacho asked.

Deb gave a tight smile. "It's more what they think of me. Most judges start as defense attorneys or prosecutors. My worthy opponent was a prosecutor before he became a judge. You know I'm a defense attorney. I'm running because he loves to throw the book at anyone who isn't a member of his country club. The cops love him and hate me. The less I have to do with them, the better."

Nacho nodded. "That's what I figured. Well, for right now, I think you'll be okay with BB. Better to get you out of here than to wait for backup."

This did not sound good to me. Keeping Deb from being blown up was not what I had been trying to do. If I had *known* there was a bomb, I would have been running just as quickly in the other direction. Trying to keep anything else from happening to Deb required knowledge, power, and fearlessness that I did not have nor did I aspire to acquire. I didn't want to play bodyguard. I'm much better in a sitting—or, even better, reclining—position, involved in nearly anything other than dodging bullets or attackers. I held up my hand, hoping the 'adults' would listen to reason. "I don't think I can be of much help. I can't exactly offer protection."

Nacho glared at me. "You don't have to protect, BB. God, I wouldn't trust you to protect my niece's honor at a Cher concert. I just need you to keep your eyes open and if you see something scary, do what you do best . . . scream like a little girl."

Deb began to object to this obviously sexist remark, but Nacho clarified, "I mean in pitch and volume. A little girl would have more composure. Once you get moving, call Roger and have him meet you at the judge's. He'll be able to handle things from there on out."

"Roger?" I asked. I didn't understand how Roger would help. He was a friend, but he didn't know any more about bombs and danger than I did. We had spent many happy evenings chasing the bottoms of bottles and boys, but beyond that....

Deb broke into my concerns. "Come on, BB," she said. "All we need to do is get to Judge Walker's house. Let me get Slasher. I don't want him to be upset by all the commotion." She popped out onto the patio and returned, stroking the dog. I had nearly been blown to pieces and now was supposed to be a target for whoever else was out there waiting to finish the job, and Deb was worried about her Chihuahua being traumatized. I began to blubber objections, but Nacho cut me off.

"The police are sure to be in here soon," Nacho said. "If you two don't slip out the back now, you ain't getting out."

Deb nodded. "Okay, BB. Time to man up. Let's go."

I sighed as the two of them stared at me with much more confidence than they should. I shrugged and that was all it took. Nacho led us to the back gate and slid it open.

I glanced back at the office. The briefcase sat on the table. Typical. I ran back and grabbed it and handed it to Deb.

She smiled. "Thanks again, BB."

"Deb. This thing nearly got me killed and saved your life. What's in it?"

She grinned. "Mostly I carry it to look official. There are a few campaign flyers and a pen. I stuck a law book in there to give it some weight. Oh, and I put a sandwich and a cookie in it today, in case I got hungry."

I shook my head. "Next time, I'm going to leave the damn thing."

"Better not. It's one of your primary functions and the one you do best."

Nacho growled, "Okay, BB, shake your butt." We squeezed through the gate and into the alley that ran along the side of *Hoosier Daddy*.

"Be back here this evening," Nacho called. "I'll have more information and we can figure out our next steps."

Deb nodded and continued to steer my unwilling feet in the direction of my car.

Chapter Two
Off We Go

I started to shake as soon as we pulled into traffic. I had almost been blown up. I tried to breathe through it and calm the fuck down, but I couldn't keep the wheel straight. Luckily for us there's not a lot of traffic in Magawatta on a Sunday afternoon.

Deb looked over at me. "Stop the car, BB," she commanded.

I did. I didn't even try to pull over. There are advantages to living in a small college town. Traffic is usually light, and people generally expect stupid driving maneuvers which involve picking up students and dodging hallucinations. Deb got out, walked to my door and opened it, pulled me up out of the seat like I was a very small bag of groceries, and walked- carried me to the passenger side. She pushed me into the seat, put Slasher in my lap, and reached across to buckle the belt. Then she walked back to the driver side and away we drove. Not a single car honked at us during this dance. I sat there and shook, trying very hard not to cry.

Looking out the windshield, giving me as much space as she could in a car much too small for a person of her personality, she spoke to the street, "Deep breaths, BB. It's over now. We are driving away and we are both in one piece. Just breathe."

I followed her commands. It was good and comforting to follow orders. Deb aimed us toward the judge's house. It was in a much better part of town full of large limestone houses that bespoke the importance of of their residents.

"Once we get there, you'll have a chance to relax, BB. However, now I need you to call Roger. I wantyou to tell him what happened so you don't talk about it when we are at the judge's house. Even if those ladies have heard about the blast, they do not need to know it had anything to do with me," Deb spoke slowly and clearly, like she was talking to a small, stupid child. I didn't take offense. "Do you understand?"

I nodded and continued to look out the windshield.

"BB."

"What?"

"I need you to call Roger. Okay?" I nodded.

"Now, BB."

"Oh, right." I found my phone in the inside breast pocket of the utilitarian sport coat I wore to all her events, hoping it added a bit of panache. The flying Deb had not crushed it. The screen was full of texts and calls. I had switched off the sound during the event and, as usual, had forgotten to turn it back on. In my regular job, I help put together special exhibits at the library on campus. Dustyn, my boss, had evidently run into a problem and was flipping out. This was not surprising, even though it was Sunday. He had major meltdowns several times a day. I have seen him turn into a gibbering mess, then sulk for most of the day because of a lack of his favorite bagel shmear—herb, no garlic, with a hint of lavender. Something at work was apparently not to his exact liking and he needed to *process* at great length. To come to a *meeting of the minds*.

I sighed. Dustyn's melodramas were not on my menu this afternoon. At the best of times, he made me want to chew my hand off as he droned on and on. Now . . . well, I dialed Roger. Good old Roger. Comfortable Roger. He would laugh at the whole thing and make some nasty remark about me being built like a brick shithouse and everything would be fine.

However, as soon as the words, 'Nacho told me to call,' were out of my mouth, a very different Roger went from sleepy to wide awake and began barking orders.

"Okay, BB. Very important. Don't stop for anything along the way. I mean anything. If there is an accident, take a side street around it but don't stop. Do you understand?"

"Why would I want to—"

"Shut up and do what I tell you. You do not stop.

No matter what. Do not stop. Do you understand?" "Okay. Geez."

Roger continued, "Now, when you get to the judge's house, park in front of the house. I don't care if there isn't a space. Double park. Do you understand?"

"But won't I get a— "

"BB, we are not having a discussion. I'm telling you what to do. Leave the car. If you are double parked, leave the keys in the car. Get out of the car first and walk to Deb's door. I'm assuming you shit the bed and she's driving."

"Well, I was a little shaken so—"

"BB. Don't explain. Follow directions. Walk to her side. Look around. If you see anyone who looks even a little suspicious, don't let her get out of the car. Wait there for me or Petunia. Got it?"

"Yes, Roger." I sighed. And I thought Beau was the melodramatic one.

"Good. If you don't see anyone, walk with Deb to the judge's house. Stay behind her. Reach around and try to open the door. It's probably open, so you can step right inside. Don't wait for someone to open the door. Open it and step inside. Make sure you stay behind Deb."

"Why?"

"You make a better target."

"But—"

"Shut up, BB. Just do it. Petunia and I will be there before the event is over and we'll take it from there. You have one job—get her from the car to the inside of the judge's house. Can you do that?"

"I guess so, but do you really think someone might be trying—"

"Goodbye, BB." He hung up.

I turned to Deb. She glanced over at me. "I heard. Don't worry, BB. Even if they're shooting at you, I'm a lot wider. They'll probably shoot around you."

It didn't make me feel better.

"Just breathe. We'll be there soon."

So that is what I did. I sat very quietly and thought of birds and springtime and went somewhere far, far away. All too soon, Deb pulled up in front of the respectable residence of Judge Walker. She looked at me. "We're here. Ready to be a bodyguard?"

Chapter Three
Judge Walker

Judge Walker lived in a stately brick edifice with columns outside. The house reeked of conservative respectability and old establishment power. It was off-putting and looked like it fully intended to be.

It was exactly the kind of place I would expect Judge Walker to live. Judge Walker was one of the most prominent and powerful people in Magawatta and a force to be reckoned with throughout the entire state of Indiana. That she had maintained her position, both socially and politically, amid the thinly veiled racism and in-your-face sexism that was rampant in the state was a testament to her personal force of will and her rock solid conservatism. She was a law and order person and rarely could be persuaded to offer a break or second chance. Having Judge Walker invite Deb to speak and possibly go so far as to endorse her candidacy was slightly more surprising than pigs sprouting wings and taking to the air. There had been no question at the beginning of the election cycle that she was certain to endorse Deb's opponent, Judge Franklin Hawthorne, who was equally conservative politically. Walker and Hawthorne were inseparable. Two immovable bookends to hard core legal opinions which favored business over people and haves over have nots. As moral and knowledgeable as Judge Walker was, Hawthorne was that much more of a lost cause. On his best days, he rose to incompetent and often languished in aggressively stupid. His saving grace was that he always knew who's lead to follow, and Judge Walker was definitely his top. He didn't complain. He was a jolly drunk and had managed to be reelected for years because he had no opinions of his own, was more than willing to do what his donors wanted, and he was a pleasant person—as long as he was sufficiently lubricated, which he invariably was. He also had a sneaky side, rarely seen, paired with a vindictive streak and a long memory for settling scores and slights, perceived or real. Those who had witnessed his devious side were rarely around long enough to share any warning. After the miscreant was eviscerated, the jolly, incompetent mask would return. This combination of exterior jolly suck up and hidden enforcer had worked for years.

However, just two weeks ago, an enterprising newspaper reporter acting on an anonymous tip discovered Judge Hawthorne at a local hotel in a drunken stupor. Hawthorne was barely clothed in fishnet stockings, a leather jockstrap, and a red rubber ball buckled into his mouth. The pictures showed a wide expanse of very white and puffy flesh. Along with the judge was an array of illegal consumables, evidently lifted from evidence and the barely legal twin sons of the local basketball coach.

The judge's career was finished. Besmirching youth was one thing. Besmirching the holy game of basketball was quite another. And while the age of the boys might have been explained away, their genitals sealed his fate. Conservatives, drugs, and homos did not mix in this very red state. Hawthorne's name would still appear on the ballot because they had already been printed, but the speed with which his supporters distanced themselves was impressive. Judge Walker had the option of endorsing no one or endorsing Deb, thus banking a favor to be redeemed later. She was not happy with her choices, but her pragmatism won over her distaste for Deb's positions —both in the courtroom and in the bedroom.

We sat in the car in front of the house. Deb finally poked me. "BB! Aren't you going to . . .?"

I had forgotten Roger's order. Deb reached over and undid my seat belt. She poked me again. "BB. Open the door for the lady."

I suddenly remembered I was supposed to be playing bodyguard. There are many things I am not suited for, and very high on the list was providing protection. I sighed, opened my door, and stepped out. I looked around. There were no obvious machine gun toting snipers that I could see. Of course, anyone who knew what they were doing would know enough to keep me from seeing them. So, I guess the only way I was going to protect Deb was to provide a different target. Fabulous.

Wondering what it would feel like to be shot, I walked around the car clutching Slasher to my chest and opened Deb's door. She stood. I handed her Slasher, then reached in the back and grabbed the briefcase. We headed to the door. Deb led the way, comforting the dog and straightening her robe. I followed, trying to mentally produce a glowing force field that would protect us from bullets or other implements of destruction. Thankfully, there was no need for my nonexistent psychic powers. We made it up the walk unscathed.

Even before we got to the door, it was opened by a middle-aged woman, her ash blond hair shot with gray pulled back into a severe bun from which not a single hair escaped. She was dressed in a dark business suit with creases sharp enough to cut steel. The woman looked us up and down with barely hidden distaste. Steel-blue eyes telegraphed her desire to dissect us quickly and throw away the pieces.

"I am Betina Leticia East, Judge Walker's personal secretary. You may call me Leticia or Ms. East. We have been expecting you. You are late." She still held the door handle in a death grip, blocking our entry. She gave us the once over again. It was a good thing there were no assassins lurking, because she was ensuring that they would have a nice, long, clear shot. I felt an itching between my shoulder blades as I imagined the scopes of a bevy of rifles being aimed there.

Deb looked back at Ms. East, daring her to say anything derogatory. Leticia's gaze fell on Slasher cuddled in Deb's arms. Her eyes widened and she opened her mouth to protest. Before she could, Deb stated in a voice that allowed no disagreement, "I never go anywhere without my dog."

It was true. Where Deb went, Slasher went, too. Slasher was more than Deb's dog. Small dogs often become part of their humans because they are always attached in some way—on the lap, in the arms, or leaning against. All those were true of Slasher. However, Slasher had also saved Deb's life. Very early one winter morning when Deb was firmly ensconced in dreamland, Slasher began to whine, bark, and perform a dance on her head. After several iterations of this routine, Deb gave in, certain that to ignore the dog would result in a very unpleasant cleanup. She stumbled downstairs to let Slasher out and found the bathroom off the kitchen quite cheerily ablaze. A wall heater had malfunctioned and caught fire. Deb had ripped down the fire alarm in that bathroom several weeks before because every time she burned something in the kitchen, it would go off. So, if Slasher had not taken drastic action, the house might well have burned. As it was, the bathroom was a total loss and Slasher was elevated from cute friend to equal partner. Few mothers could match the love and devotion Deb held for that dog.

Ms. East did not know this history, but she knew a battle of wills when she saw it. She was the gatekeeper to her personal holiest of holies, Judge Walker. The idea of allowing this sacred site to be besmirched by an animal was an unallowable horror. However, she could hardly deny Deb entry. Judge Walker wanted this disreputable woman to appear. Ms. East could not deny the Judge's wishes. With a supreme effort of will, Ms. East caved. Lips pressed tightly together in disapproval, she nodded slightly and stepped back, allowing us entry. She stopped a few feet from the door and gestured to a small room off the hallway. "The judge is in the library with her guests. Wait here and I will tell her you have finally arrived."

She was obviously not going to move until she saw us safely seated, not trusting us to roam the house. With a final look at the three outsider creatures who, she obviously anticipated, would desecrate all they touched, she turned and left.

Deb looked at me, a smile playing on her face. "I just wish Slasher would poop on command," she said. "If there was ever a situation that called for an accident "

"And I would be blamed, not the dog," I said. "Keep those thoughts to yourself. Judge Walker won't endorse you, no matter what your opponent did, if your little Slasher leaves an offering."

"You're right, BB. But a girl can dream."

Further dreaming was halted by the arrival of Judge Walker, Leticia hovering just behind her. "Miss Eubank, thank you for coming," the judge said, holding out her hand. "I am Shirley Walker. May I have a few words before we go in?"

Deb stood, handing Slasher to me and picking up the briefcase. She shook the judge's hand. Deb and the judge both knew that it was Deb who was receiving the boon. An invitation to appear before the *Ladies' Garden and Debate Society*—the bastion of the genteel power elite in town—was practically an endorsement by itself, even if the judge said nothing. Here, on a monthly basis, the most powerful women in town, some by marriage, some by their own accomplishment—not to say that marrying and staying with the moldering wreckages of physical and moral humanity who ruled the roost in our little hen house was not an awesome accomplishment—met, drank, and decided on the needs and direction of Magawatta. We never dreamed that Deb would be invited here, but then again, we had never dreamed of Judge Hawthorne's photo spread, either.

Deb nodded briefly. "Sure. What's on your mind?"

"You know that barring any more surprises, we are nearly certain to be members of the same court after the election. I have always had a productive working relationship with my fellow judges and while I understand you and I have different interpretations of the law, I hope that we will be able to talk out our differences. We are certain to disagree, but I do not wish to go to war. That will not serve you, me, the court, or justice. Do you agree?"

Deb thought a bit, studying the judge closely. Finally, she decided. She nodded. "You're right. We aren't going to agree. However, I have respect for you even when I disagree with you. As long as we keep an open pipeline and I get as much respect as I give, then we can work together."

Judge Walker gave a tight smile. "Then I believe we have an understanding that we can both live with." She gestured toward the library. "The ladies in here are conservative, but caring. They know enough to understand there are two sides to every issue. When they ask how you will rule, I suggest you stick to the mantra that your decision depends on the case. They know your politics, but this is not politics. This is the law. If the discussion gets too far into politics, I will stop it and steer us back to how to judge. Is that acceptable?"

Deb nodded and actually smiled. "You're not as —"

Judge Walker held up a hand. "Please. We shall not be friends. We will be colleagues. Is that understood and acceptable?"

Not to be flummoxed by her rules, Deb swept the judge up in a big hug. "Shirl . . . you and I are gonna have some big fun together. Just you wait and see."

Stunned, the judge, who I suspected never allowed her personal space to be so invaded, pulled herself together as well as she could. "Well. Then please, come and meet the ladies."

They headed back down the hall toward the meeting, and I followed.

However, a handful of talon-like nails dug into my shoulder and pulled me back. Leticia East hissed at me, "You and that *thing*," she nodded toward Slasher, "will wait here."

I looked toward Deb, but she shrugged and mouthed, "Let it go."

The judge said, "Leticia, why don't you keep our guest company?"

The woman gave a little gasp of protest. She obviously did not want to lower herself to commune with the likes of me. "But, won't you need me to . . ." she began.

"I'm sure I can handle things," the judge replied and continued down the hall, leading Deb away.

Leticia sank into a chair and glared at me as if I and the dog had soiled not only the rug, but her life, too. She did not offer a chair. I knew it was out of the question to get anything like a drink. I didn't care. There had been far too much excitement packed into far too little time for this little boy. I sat, hugging Slasher, rubbing his soft fur and let my eyes close. I wanted nothing more than to drift away to a lovely warm place in my mind where sea breezes cooled me and glistening native boys rubbed my aching shoulders.

"I don't think she should be in there without me," Leticia blurted.

I opened my eyes, torn away from my island paradise. Leticia was actually twitching as she sat, gazing mournfully at the doorway, torn between her desire to safeguard her boss from anything untoward and said boss's explicit instructions to stay.

"She depends on me, you know," she said defensively. "I'm always there for her. Anything could happen with that woman here."

"That woman?" I asked, opening my eyes. This lady was definitely looking to have me read her beads. But Leticia was lost in her own mental meltdown. Her eyes kept straying to the door before returning to me. It was rather entertaining to watch. Her eyes filled with dreamy concern as they drifted to the door. And as they returned to me, disgust made her eyes narrow and nose wrinkle. It was like she was watching a game of catch between a deity and a pile of poo. There was a bit of pleasure in knowing that my mere presence forced her to remain here and worry about what I might do. Perhaps she thought I would begin to rub my gayness on the furniture and drapes. It was a pleasure to be able to irritate her without expending any effort. It takes a big man not to take advantage of such a situation . . . and I am not a big man.

I stood and set Slasher on the chair, earning me a hiss of disapproval from Ms. East. I began to wander around the room, looking at some of the objet d'art. Most had obviously been selected by a queer decorator hired to add culture to a lifeless space. On a small table near the door, a stunning antique lotion pump caught my attention. It's simplicity appealed to me, as did the translucent blue of the bottle. Moreover, the scent that rose from a drop of lotion that clung to its dispenser was sublime. I am not known for my taste in clothes or men. Roger would say that I am known for my bad taste in both. However, in the arena of lovely smells, my gay flag flies proudly. I can distinguish between a wide variety of popular creams, colognes, perfumes, and eau de toilets. I can pick the best scent for the best impression. I can distinguish quality from marketing. It is one of the things that gives me pleasure and pride. It also gives me a bit of a headache when around popular, but inferior products so common among the young.

This lotion was one I had never inhaled before and it was lovely. A light crush of lavender, a hint of sage, and an impeccable base lotion blended to perfection. I had to try some. I picked up the pump, enjoying the weight in my hand, and moved to sample a squirt. Leticia leapt up and snatched the bottle from my hand.

"No!" she hissed. "No one but the judge uses that lotion. No one!" She carefully replaced the bottle on the table as if laying baby Jesus back into his crib. "The judge has it made especially for her in France. It is her own personal scent, and no one is to use it but her . . ." she looked at the bottle with reverence, "not even me." She looked at me, longing in her eyes. "I can, of course, smell it on the items the judge has touched. But no one can use the lotion." She looked at me fiercely. "*No one.*"

I held up my hands in surrender. I didn't mind poking the bull from the safety of the bleachers, but I wasn't going to get right down in the ring and dance with crazy. I went back to my chair, picked up Slasher, and began to stroke his coat. Leticia sat back down and glared at me from across the room. I ignored her and let my eyes close again, drifting back to my island retreat and native boys.

"It seems that your candidate will be victorious." Leticia spoke, pulling me back from my happy fantasy yet again. If I hadn't disliked her before . . . but she had something on her mind. "That means we will be working together extensively, and I want to set some ground rules."

"Working together?" I asked. "What makes you think that?"

"You are Ms. Eubank's advisor. You direct what she does, who she meets, where she goes. That is what I do with Judge Walker. Ours is a position of great responsibility and power."

I could swear she let out a little moan of pleasure when she said that. This was taking a decidedly kinky turn.

"What do you mean? *They* are the judges."

"But we control who can see them. Who gets access. When they go and where they go. We are the keepers of the schedule. We, who are never noticed, hold the reins."

I swear, she was starting to breathe heavily. She fingered a little golden cross at her neck. "They are the valiant beasts, but we have the reins and we ride them." She looked at me. "So you and I must come to some agreements as to how we shall direct our thoroughbreds."

I stood, moving toward the door. This was too disturbing. Judge Walker had a dedicated whack job as her assistant. I turned to her. "Look, Ms. East, it may be true that we will be working together a bit. I'm not sure what role I'll be taking on after the election. I hadn't really thought about it. I already have a job. But let me clarify. Deb is not someone I have any ability or desire to strap a set of reins on. She is and always has been a force unto herself. If she ever suspected I was trying to control access to her, she would hurt me in unspeakable ways. Besides, control is not on my wish list. Nice shoes, outfits that attract interested glances, young men hungering to be near me—sure. But control of the seamier side of Magawatta politics? No way. So, I believe this conversation, although oddly intriguing, needs to end. It is time for me to go." I stepped toward the door and ran into Deb's bulk. She was in a foul mood. She grabbed me. "Come on, BB. Time to go talk to some real people."

We headed toward the main door. Judge Walker stepped into the hall.

"Miss Eubank," she called. Deb stopped and turned.

"I am sorry that went as it did. You are a surprising woman."

Deb opened her mouth to retort, but the judge held up her hand.

"I do not mean that in a derogatory manner. What you just did impressed me. We may not see eye to eye on cases in the future, but you have the backbone to stand for what you believe is right. I cannot ask for more. I look forward to working with you and the many arguments I am sure we will have."

She turned and went back into the meeting. Leticia stood and ushered us toward the door, obviously anxious to hurry back to her boss and see what damages the upstart had caused. Deb's lips were pressed together. Mama was not happy but wasn't going to say anything until we got out of there. She handed me her briefcase and took Slasher, holding the little dog close, allowing him to lick her face. Then we both followed Leticia to the door. She let us out and slammed the door. I could hear it lock. I could only hope this was the last we'd see of Ms. Betina Leticia East and I'm sure the feeling was mutual.

"What went wrong with the judge?" I asked.

"She *introduced* me but didn't endorse me. Said she felt it imperative she remain impartial. So, when I win, I owe her, but if anything untoward happens, she can claim she never wanted me."

"Not nice," I said, "but pretty smart."

"Then the ladies started grilling me," Deb continued. "We didn't find a single position where they agreed with me. They would love to support anyone else."

"Will they vote for Hawthorne?"

She smiled. "I don't think so. I can also tell that the idea of not voting really bothers them. They are the power elite. Not using their power is like not using their platinum card to impress whoever is watching. I think they'll hold their noses and vote for me, but then loudly criticize everything I do to their friends, agreeing that I duped them. That way they can announce that they voted, that they gave the other side a try. And the radical dyke disappointed, just as they expected I would."

"So, a wonderful time was had by all," I said.

"I hope I never have to see those people again," Deb said. "Unless they are standing in front of me in court and I'm judging them."

"Instead of visa versa," I said.

At the curb, Roger's car had pulled up beside mine and double parked. He was standing in front of my car, scanning the area. Petunia, dressed as always in black leather, long, dark ponytail pulled back and wound with what looked like barbed wire, leaned on the rear panel. She looked like she dismembered professional wrestlers for exercise and entertainment. I had seen her smile once before. Thinking of it now, my legs instinctively squeezed together for protection.

Roger pivoted toward us. "Looks clear for now. Come on you two. We have a meeting with Nacho. There's strategy to plan."

Deb leaned forward and gave Petunia a quick peck on the cheek, then reached around and gave her ass a squeeze. I held my breath, expecting Petunia to reach out and disembowel her without another word. Instead she gave Deb a quick hug and gently bit her ear. It was like watching two T-Rexes cuddle—cute and disturbing at the same time.

Before anything else could be said, three police cars pulled up, lights flashing, blocking the street. In Magawatta, anything that rated police presence seemed to require at least three cars. Roger had explained it once, "They need three cars. One to do something. One to watch. One to go for doughnuts. And all but the most senior cops need to have a partner with them to carry a spare set of keys when the driver forgets and locks his inside."

Four officers piled out, hands on weapons, alert and ready. The lead officer, Detective Crawford, stepped up to Deb.

He nodded his greeting. "Deb."

She was equally polite but distant. "Detective."

"Seems you had a little car trouble back downtown."

"Oh?"

"Come on, Deb. You know someone blew up your truck. I know you were there and left the scene. You also know that we aren't going to let something like that happen without an investigation. We need to talk to you. Why don't we all drive over to the station and get this over with?"

"And if I say this isn't a good time?"

"I will politely ask you to make it a good time. Otherwise, I will have to be an asshole and cite you for leaving the scene of an accident and take you with me."

Deb smiled. "Aw, Crawford, you say the sweetest things. I believe my friend BB would be happy to drop me by the station on his way home." She turned to me. "Could you drop me off, BB?"

She gave me a look. I realized that she did not want me to make a statement. That was fine with me. I never was good at cops and robbers. When I was a kid, I always got stuck being the robber and never got away with anything. Of course, that did mean that Joshy Huffman would tackle me and punish me, which made it worthwhile, but now that I had put away childish things . .

I nodded. "Sure, Deb. I can do that. When?"

The Detective said, "Now would be convenient. How about I lead the way and Sargent Johnson follows, just to make sure you don't get lost?"

Roger spoke quietly to just us, "We'll meet at Nacho's at six. You'll be finished by then." Deb nodded. We all got into our cars and had a little parade down the street to the police station.

In the car, Deb said. "If they ask, you are just my ride. You did not see the truck blow up. You did not see me near my truck. You picked me up at the bar and drove me here. The truck must have blown up as we were leaving or after we left. You heard a bang, but didn't know what it was."

"Why? Why not say what had happened?"

"Because they would love to make this look like an attack—"

"Which it was," I broke in.

"Which it *might have been*, but if they make that decision, they are going to limit my appearances. They will make it look like I'm a dangerous person and if I'm elected, Magawatta can expect to become the bombing capitol of the Western world. I am *not* going to let that happen. So, repeat the story to me." She gave me a dangerous look. "Now!"

I did. She made me repeat it a few more times.

By that time, we were at the station.

"Pull over in front. Let me out and then leave. Take Slasher with you. I'll call when I'm done and you can come get me. Don't wait around here. You have long-lost cousins waiting at home—or need to feed your plants. Just don't get out and talk to them. Do you understand?"

I nodded, pulled over, and let her out. She handed Slasher to me, waved, and called out, "Thanks, BB. See you sometime. Don't forget to say hi to Cousin Dora for me."

Then she turned and walked into the station. I pulled away from the curb with the extreme caution one uses when driving near a policeman. Then I headed home. I was happy to follow orders. This Dorothy was ready to go back to Kansas and perhaps dream a little dream of Oz.

Chapter Four
Sunday Night

The same group of reprobates regularly gathered on Sunday evenings to enjoy TiaRa del Fuego's *Parade of Gowns* drag show, which burst into being every Sunday evening from eight until midnight, filling *Hoosier Daddy* with performance and song. Before the show and between sets, we spent the evening chatting, catting, bullshitting and leering, all to the accompaniment of drinks aplenty and many platefuls of Nacho's exquisite nachos.

This evening, however, our usual repertoire was set aside for a serious discussion of what to do. The excitement of that afternoon's rally for Deb had been eclipsed by the explosion of Boomer and the near- death of Deb and me. As an indication of the importance of our discussion, Nacho had left the kitchen and joined us. This was a first. Nacho always spent the evening in the kitchen, coming out only to deliver orders when the crowd was too much for Jackie, the current studlet in waiting, to handle.

As I walked up to the table, signaling to Jackie that a drink was definitely in order, Beau's face lit up. "Ah, BB, I hear you've taken a turn to the butch.

Facing bombs and whisking the damsel in distress away from danger. Soon you'll be pounding back brewskies and scratching yourself in public." Beau was my oldest friend in town. A blushing Southern dingbat whose swirling lassitude was tempered only by an abject terror of having to return to live with his born-again, homophobic clan, lived down the block from me.

We had met years ago when we had taken the

same short-lived job as tutors for student services. We had both been over-qualified and cared far more about the material than our tutees did. Neither of us was willing to accept the money or, upon occasion, the sex offered by the tutees to just do the work for them. The job had ended after a semester, but our friendship had not. Beau sometimes drank a bit more than was opportune but was still a reliable friend.

Roger snorted. "Hardly. If he'd known about the bomb, he would have run the other way. As for the whisking, the only thing he provided was a convenient car. If Deb wasn't there to keep him calm, he'd probably still be in some corner soiling himself."

"Can it you two," Nacho growled. "I ain't got time for your babble. There's news. There's plans to be made. Plus, I still got a place to run and it don't run itself."

"Where's Deb?" I asked.

"Still at the cop shop," Roger answered. "Petunia's there, loitering outside, probably scaring all the little boys in blue, and will bring her here when Detective Crawford is finished with her."

"Starting tonight, I want her watched," Nacho said. "I heard from my people. That bomb was made by a professional, like I thought."

"Your people?" Beau asked. "Who are your people, and how could they find out something that sensitive that quickly? Nacho, I know you can do things in the kitchen I could never dream of trying to recreate and your word is law here . . . but what exactly—"

Aunt May placed a hand on her nephew's arm. "Beauregard, do not ask questions which may provide you with information that carries too heavy a burden. You know I am quite fond of you, but you must admit to a certain difficulty in keeping your mouth closed, particularly when you have been indulging on the more liquid side of entertainments. It has been my observation that the more libations you have enjoyed, the wilder and juicier the tidbits that leak from your mouth become. You simply cannot control your tongue." Her eyes lost focus.

"I remember Thaddeus Bucknell had a similar weakness. However, I did not mind that failing with him, as I was the juicy tidbit he sought and his mouth was not open to let things out of but to place things into, and the control he had over his tongue . . . well, it was masterful."

Aunt May looked ancient and proper, the perfect Southern lady. But when she unwrapped her hand from around the stem of her ever-present drink, patted her lips, and began to speak, the illusion was shattered. She had been moved to live with Beau many years ago when her reminisces about now married and respectable men became too constant an embarrassment for Louisiana society.

Beau stepped in to stop the flow of verbiage. "Thank you for that image, Aunt May, but I don't understand. Why not enjoy a bit of tea about Nacho?"

Nacho broke in, "No tea for you, Beau. If I need you to know something, I'll tell you. Otherwise ... "

The glower Nacho pointed his way was deadly enough to penetrate even Beau's Sunday afternoon haze. Beau did not have Aunt May's ability to maintain under the influence, but he did share her thirst. However, he possessed an over-educated wit and a kind nature, so his occasional over indulgences were overlooked.

Impatient, Nacho continued, "I've sent out word for some helpers, but it will take a couple of days. So, Roger, I'm relying on you and Petunia."

I protested, "I understand Petunia, but Roger? What can he do? Provide biting commentary? Besides, shouldn't we rely on the professionals? Isn't this the kind of thing the police are for?"

"They don't know it yet, but I got a notion this is out of their league," Nacho said. "Until we find who's gunning for Deb, I'm not going to trust a force that mostly focuses on keeping drunk frats and locals from killing each other. I have some experts looking into it, but that will take time. Until then, we got to keep her safe, which brings us back to you, Roger."

"Wait a minute," I protested. "Why Roger? I *know* I'm of no use. According to you, the police don't have the chops. But Roger? And why did you call Roger this afternoon? What's going on?"

Roger was one of my oldest friends. We shared a love of the young and tight, and a taste in humor that ran toward the gutter. We had spent many pleasant evenings mixing drinks and partners with the comfort of friends who had absolutely no sexual interest in the other. He was a master of the all-knowing Mr. Nasty proclamation, and we often engaged in enjoyable arguments over topics neither cared much about. However, I knew little about his work life. Whenever I brought it up—which was rarely, as work in our world was a necessary evil, but not an interesting topic of discussion—he would dismiss any questions, saying, "If I wanted to think about work, I'd be doing it." I believed he sold things on the internet and "solved problems". However, this was a completely different kettle of fish.

Nacho looked at Roger significantly.

Roger sighed. "BB, you might as well know. I do have an occupation. It is why I know Petunia. She is my employee."

"Your employee? You mean you own a company?"

He nodded. "Mostly I coordinate. I don't have to take part in the actual cases anymore."

“Cases?"

He looked uncomfortable, which was rare. Roger never looked uncomfortable.

"Yes. Well, there's no easy way to say it. I own a small consulting agency that provides investigations of a very discrete nature for a very small, loyal, and powerful group of clients. When something needs to be found out or not found out, without any hint of what was being looked into slipping out, they call me."

I looked at him blankly. This didn't make any sense. "You do what?"

Beau, with degrees in literature and philosophy and a vast library of trivial information both in hard copy and floating around his head, split his face with a grin that would have put the Cheshire cat to shame. "Oh, could it be?" he asked, his eyes twinkling in delight. "Our dear Roger, whose very existence seems to celebrate being a public dick—in every sense of the word—is actually a very private dick?"

"Huh?"

"A detective, BB. Roger is a private detective."

I was stunned. "No, that's not possible." I looked at Roger, expecting a joke of some kind. Instead, his face was painted with a rueful smile. "I never suspected . . ." I began.

Roger shrugged. "That's kind of the point, BB. I'm discrete. Unless someone absolutely has to know, they don't."

I was speechless.

Nacho reached over and slapped my back. "Don't worry about it, cupcake. The sheer volume of things you don't know is staggering. Now you have a smidge more on the 'do know' side of the scales. I still think you'd rather let Roger volunteer for guard duty since there's an unknown assassin on the loose."

That gave me pause. My version of courage is wearing a particularly daring shade of eyeliner on a night out or a shirt that might be considered by the unkind a bit tight for a man of my physique.

"No one is following me or protecting me and that's final!" Deb proclaimed, barreling up to the table. That she had made it through the doors onto the patio and up to our table without exciting our notice was an indication of the shock value of Roger's revelation. While we always paid attention to the discussion at hand, the eyes of all at the table were constantly roaming. Who knows when a tight young thing might drop a set of keys or spill something somewhere that begged to be wiped up?

However, Deb now was towering over us, an impressive feat as she was not a tall tower. However, strength of will, heightened by agitation and topped with anger, added to her height considerably.

"I have just spent three hours being probed and prodded by that idiot Crawford. Now you want to put a security detail around me? Are you nuts? I'm a big girl, Nacho. I've had enemies and dealt with threats. I'm used to it. I'm not going to give them the satisfaction . . ." She took Slasher from me, sat down, and glared at Nacho. "It doesn't surprise me that BB is freaked, but I'd expected better from you."

Nacho didn't blink and glared right back at her. "Deb, you've been a big fish in a small pond around here for a long time. But you're aiming for waters a lot bigger than you can imagine. You ain't dumb, but you're actin' dumb. Stop tryin' to out butch everyone at the table. I *know* you got a backbone. We all know. But this is more than any one person can handle. We still don't know what's goin' on, but the more I find out, the more it stinks."

Deb did not like giving up control. However, she was also a master at assessing situations. We all suspected that Nacho had untold connections and resources. All of us followed any orders Nacho gave without question if for no other reason than to ignore them might result in being banned from the *Café*.

Deb stared at Nacho for a minute longer, then nodded.

"Escort to events, but no surveillance at home," she said. "I don't want to have to worry about clearing it if Slasher or I want to go outside to take a pee at night." Deb lived on the outskirts of town in an extensively remodeled log house. She valued her privacy and there were acres surrounding the place. She looked around the table. "What do we know?"

Roger spoke up, "What do the police think?"

Deb rolled her eyes. "They are focusing on my private life. They suspect my ex."

"Carmen?" I asked. "Why?"

"The breakup was less than cordial. Carmen has a temper and has had some, shall I say, *interactions* with the authorities before. There was a protest where she threatened to shove some Nazi's head up his ass so far he could see what he had for breakfast. We were still together at the time, and I convinced the young man that pressing charges would also entail broadcasting the story of how he had been intimidated by a mere woman."

"Mere woman," Roger laughed. "There is nothing *mere* about Carmen. She's been teaching martial arts since she was twenty."

"The other issue," Deb continued with a smile, "is that she works at Crane."

"The Naval station that protects Southern Indiana's vital coastline?" I asked. "What difference does that make?"

"Since there isn't an ocean or even a lake in the area, Crane is a munitions depot. They store and decommission a whole lot of ordinance there. In short, Carmen likes to blow things up and she's good at it."

"Makes sense," Nacho said. "She knows about bombs. Crawford sees a powerful lesbian who knows bombs and don't like you, and he sees a lovers' spat."

"Sounds like a good promo for a porno," Roger said.

"I do believe I could come up with a more visually stimulating fantasy, given the same cast of characters," Aunt May said, her eyes looking off into the distance, obviously developing a story line.

Beau touched her shoulder to bring her attention back to the matter at hand. "Ah, yes," Aunt May said, "I suppose the question is, could she have applied her knowledge to blowing up your truck?"

"Could or would?" Deb asked, ready to defend Carmen. "We might have split, but I'd like to think I am a good enough judge of people to know that even after breaking up, she wasn't and isn't the type of person who would want to blow up Boomer or me for that matter."

"Who knows what evil lurks in the hearts of women scorned," Petunia said, walking up to the table. "But I have an answer as to her ability."

We looked at her. Petunia was not one to speak unless absolutely necessary. I had a tickle of anticipation. Were we about to find out something personal about the heavily guarded castle that was Petunia? But it was not to be.

"I occasionally teach a safety course out there. Reduces the number of fatalities. Carmen was in one of them. She knows how to dismantle a few things without blowing herself up, but that's as far as her knowledge goes. No knowledge or interest in building anything sophisticated. She knows how to follow procedure for blowing up existing ordinance and liked doing it. Who wouldn't? But she showed no interest in experimentation—at least, as far as bombs were concerned."

Nacho nodded. With anyone else, except Roger, Nacho would need more information. But Petunia was as reliable as gravity.

Deb spoke up, "The father of my children has the knowledge and might have the desire. He's never forgiven me for leaving him. But he never leaves his farm near Jasper. He hates Magawatta. He says it's 'full to the tits with hippies and fags'. I suggested Crawford might check into his whereabouts, but there was no interest." She turned to Nacho. "It's been a long day. I've been campaigning since ten this morning. I've done speeches and met the damn garden club and spent too long talking to an idiot. I have a rental car being delivered to my cabin this evening. I called a cab and they just texted me. Now I'm taking my dog and going home. If I see any one of you trying to follow me or stake me out or any other well-meaning act, I will very sweetly shoot you. Understood?" She looked around the table.

I held up my hands, happy to be let off the hook.

She smiled.

"BB, I had no concerns about you." Then she looked at Nacho. "Am I clear?"

Nacho was not happy but nodded. "You're checking yourself out against doctor's orders."

"I am aware of that, but Doctor Nacho, I am still going." She stood, looking at me. "BB, I have a speech at the law school tomorrow at one. I can handle that on my own. Tomorrow night is the Meet the Candidates event at the *Butler Community Center*. Let's meet at my office at six and we'll head over there. Okay?"

"We should have more information by then. Come here so we can compare notes," Nacho said.

Deb looked like she was going to protest. The prospect of another battle of wills loomed, but the events of the day had tired her out. "All right." She sighed. "BB, we'll meet here instead."

I nodded. "If you need anything before then—"

"I'll call," she said. She looked around the table. "I appreciate your help and your concern. Really, I do. But I am not scared. I will not be scared. Let's move past this." Then, hugging Slasher to her chest, she headed for the door.

Nacho waited until she was gone and turned to Roger. "You can keep an eye on her without her knowing, right?"

Roger looked offended. "I installed her security, Nacho. And even if I hadn't ..."

Nacho nodded. "Best get there before her."

Roger stood and nodded to us. "Tomorrow at five to compare notes before she gets here?"

Nacho grunted. "Sooner, if you find out anything important. Stay in touch. She's not worried, but I am."

That bothered me. Nacho could face down Armageddon and not stop stirring whatever was cooking for the denizens of the *Patio Café*. Nacho worried meant I should be running as fast as I could for as long as my less-than-well-muscled legs could carry me. The only thing that stopped me was that I had absolutely no idea which way to run and doubted either Nacho or Roger would provide any useful information other than to suggest I take a run up a part of my anatomy not made for foot traffic. I sighed and remained where I was.

Roger noticed my discomfort and I could see him consider the pleasure of adding to my distress and fears. That he did not take advantage of such an easy target also warned me of major unpleasantness afoot. He merely said, "Later days." Then he and Petunia headed out.

Nacho stood and glared first at me and then Beau. "Not a word about this to anyone. I won't ask for a promise. Just know that you will regret it more than anything you have ever regretted if any hint of this leaks out, ever. I've got work to do. I still think there are bigger over not gettin' Deb bush." Not waiting for a response, Nacho headed for the kitchen.

Beau and I looked at each other at a loss for words. Aunt May, however, knew what to do. "I believe," she said, "it is time for cocktails. Perhaps several."

I have always believed in respecting the superior knowledge of my elders. We proceeded to get appropriately plowed.

Chapter Five
Monday

I recently got a job helping to put on special exhibits at the Valentine Library on campus. The library has an enormous collection of quasi-medical books and vintage advertising materials. Dr. Winslow Valentine, who long ago gave a boat load of cash to fund the original library, had made his fortune selling patent medicines to the unsuspecting masses. Electric belts for "man problems", tape worms for women dieting, cocaine and morphine syrup for teething children, and Meat Juice Tonic for everyone who could gag it down had filled his coffers in the era before quackery was illegal and income tax was a socialist pipe dream. Since the original endowment, wise investments allowed a continued amassing of books, along with dusty and renown academics who bestowed a less sordid reputation upon the library. To keep the collections in the public eye, placate past donors and encourage those with new-found wealth to buy a bit of respectability, the high and mighty regularly decided to dust off something usually hidden away from mere mortals and with much pomp, circumstance, press, people, and photo ops, whip it out for adoring and hopefully cash laden bibliophiles. I was not in charge of such observances. Heaven forbid. Dustyn, the master of these extravaganzas, was a professional poof who absolutely lived for meditations upon the correct rituals of display, the perfect color schemes for banners, and the overall spectacle of the opening ceremonies. I fulfilled the roles of gopher and acolyte. I kept my head down and did as I was told while attempting to look interested as Dustyn bemoaned the difficulties of his exertions. In truth, I spent most of my time trying not to yawn or laugh. The job paid better than many I have had because Dustyn felt that the size of his budget indicated the esteem in which he was held. There was a minimal amount of heavy lifting, either mental or physical, so I hoped to hold on to this one for a while. If that meant stroking Dustyn's ego—and only his ego, in case you were wondering—then so be it.

The next morning, I was a tad late and in desperate need of a third cup of coffee. The evening had stretched on a bit beyond what was wise, as was often the case when I spent time with Aunt May and Beau. I can handle my liquor, but those two Southern belles had a capacity that could not be equaled. Despite that knowledge, the travails I had endured encouraged me to attempt to keep up with them. The dawn brought regrets and firm commitments to never be so foolhardy again. I knew such commitments were lies, but I was only lying to myself and I am well practiced at so violating my trust and am very forgiving, particularly when in a fraught or fragile mood.

Dustyn was on a tear about his latest opus—the unveiling of a collection of first editions of Freud in the original German. He was going on and on about the *great importance of the collection, you understand, my dear*, and the necessity of providing a sober yet uplifting color scheme and graphic ensemble to match the occasion. I understand that aficionados de gay are known for their firm grasp on all things artistic. I, however, am completely lacking in such areas. Roger often told me I was homosexually impaired. For all the fashion sense I possess, I might as well be a straight man. In fact there are obvious similarities. Like most straight men, I am obsessed with dick. The only difference is that the object of my interest lies—or stands— beneath another's belt instead of my own. But I digress.

That morning, I had no attention, interest, or words. Thankfully, Dustyn had more than enough for the both of us. All that was required from me was an occasional grunt that was at a timbre high enough to indicate rapturous fascination in the ceaseless flow of thoughts and words he was pouring forth all over us. I allowed the verbiage to gush past with not the slightest interest in dipping in a finger or thought. Dustyn needed no encouragement. As long as I was not foolish enough to express anything less than rapture or, heaven forbid, question his decisions, everything was glorious.

I knew that Deb didn't need me today. She usually could and did handle most of the heavy lifting of the campaign, such as it was. Running for judge was not exactly a demanding exercise. There were a few speeches to groups of barely awake, semi- interested neighborhood activists, mostly who were concerned with having an opportunity to beat their own dead horse. The occasional meet and greets with groups of the powers that were or at least, thought they were, such as yesterday's *Garden Club and Debate Society*, are essentially large barter sessions. 'I'll tell people you are worthy if you'll kiss some part of my body either now or at some point in the future.'

As Magawatta is a college town, there were the de rigueur talks to classes when a prof needed a break and chose a live "slice of the real world" instead of showing a film. Deb was more than able to handle those without me. What made her campaign unique was that she also held rallies with supporters. Historically, judges never had rallies. The reason for this was simple—judges rarely had supporters beyond a few in the legal or criminal professions. The usual campaign involved wrapping themselves in the solemnity of the office—in other words, the candidates were too anti-social to want to mix with mere mortals and their few supporters didn't particularly wish to mix with them. Deb was different. She held rallies with food and games and dancing on the weekends when people needed a bit of fun. She liked people, liked being with people, and liked encouraging people to stand up and speak their minds. The weekend before the election, we planned an extensive outreach. Supporters were going to knock on almost every door in Magawatta. This level of activity was unheard of and was the reason she actually needed me to help. However, during the week, the campaign went into low gear. Deb practiced law and I practiced staying awake while listening to Dustyn.

The day passed slowly enough that by quitting time, I had sufficiently recovered from yesterday's excitement of being nearly blown up and the later ablution with too many too strong liquids. I was ready, if not willing, to face whatever Roger and Nacho had dug up. I sincerely hoped they had discovered that Boomer had exploded because of a bad carburetor or a mechanic who had been shamed by Deb's superior knowledge of automobiles. I can't say I was ready for anything—I never am—but who is really? However, fear and a desire to hide had been replaced by a growing curiosity. It really didn't make sense. Who would want to risk the attention and punishment brought on by attempted murder in order to scare off or kill Deb?

With curiosity tempting the cat, I headed to *Hoosier Daddy*. From the outside, the bar is a dark and seedy place off an alley, just like so many gay bars in small, less than welcoming towns. Once inside, well, it is still dark and seedy. The back room is large and boasts a real live 70's era disco dance floor with horribly scuffed plastic panels, barely allowing colored lights to shine through. What elevates *Daddy's* from dive to fabulous is TiaRa del Fuego's drag shows and the patio café, run and ruled by Nacho Mama who makes the best nachos this side of heaven. Nacho is a force to be obeyed without question and is the keeper of many secrets. I knew some, but I doubt anyone knew all . . . at least no one still breathing. Nacho is a mystery like the Sphinx, the location of Ark of the Covenant or the actual amount of work Cher has had done, best left unknown because possessing such knowledge would surely end in tears and peril.

So, comfortably ensconced in my ignorance but with a tingle of anticipation, I turned down the alley. At the same moment, I saw Deb enter from the opposite end, Slasher tucked under her arm. I felt a certain thrill of being in tune with the universe. Our internal clocks were synchronized. The thrill was short lived as someone else crashed our party. As I raised my hand to wave, another figure turned into the alley behind her, hurrying to catch up and called, "Debbie Do."

I was close enough to see Deb's face. She had been smiling as she approached, but upon hearing the stranger's call, her face morphed into a horrific mask. I was reminded of stone idols looming above alters used for human sacrifice. She was turning, so I did not get the full impact of the look. That probably saved me from being reduced to ash. The glare did not seem to affect the large stranger who was hurrying toward her, bringing a hand out from behind his back. There was something in his hand, and I didn't think it was a bouquet of pansies.

It was a short-handled shotgun.

Now, in books and movies, the hero throws himself at the intended victim and pulls the fragile young thing out of the way just in the nick of time. The hero does not think, they act. It is an instinctual action that saves the day and the sweet young thing. Unfortunately, my hero instinct is maladjusted and what I did was close my eyes and cover my head with my hands—my go-to response. Yes, I know. Against a gun, this gallant act would be of little or no help. But instincts are devoid of thought and so was I. No spandex S stretched across rippling muscles on this boy's chest.

Fortunately, before the stranger could point the gun, Petunia, with the force and speed of a runaway freight train, barreled around the corner and slammed into him. Knocking the gun into the street, she belted him in the face with a huge fist. Even from several feet away, I heard the crunch of bone. Blood spurted from his nose. However, he did not go down. That was a shock. Petunia could knock me over by waving her arm in my direction. She could force me to my knees with a glare. This man just stood there, hand to his gushing nose, and stared at her, considering. His intellect obviously did not match his strength. He was having trouble understanding how something less than a tank had managed to stop him. Petunia drew back a massive arm, preparing to pummel him into pulp.

"Petunia! Stop!" Deb shouted.

Reluctantly, but unable to ignore the command in Deb's voice, Petunia froze, fist raised like a hammer, John Henry, ready to pound that steel on down.

At that moment, a gaggle of giggling queens poured out the door of *Daddy's,* probably to gossip and smoke. They took one look at the tableau before them, shrieked as one, and hurried back inside.

None of us moved. Blood continued to flow freely from the man's nose. If I lost that much blood, I'd be ready for embalming, but he only looked vaguely annoyed as he glared at Petunia. Then he looked at Deb and his expression changed. I may not be an astute reader of micro expressions, but it didn't matter in this case. Anger had been nurtured over many moons and been allowed to flower into a deep river of loathing, but tinged with a bit of Could it be? A bit of lust? Confused, I looked at Deb.

Her face mirrored the man's expression. Her free hand twitched, unconsciously wanting to be back in a familiar position locked around his neck. Looking back at the man, I saw similar twitches in the hand not held to his bloody nose. As a master of the obvious, I could tell that this was not the first time these two had met. Emotions this deep were not possible without long experience and interaction.

The man tore his glare away from Deb and turned back to Petunia. He motioned to the gun with his chin. "Ain't right to leave a gun on the ground like that. Ain't respectful." He was more upset about that than his broken nose.

Without moving, Petunia called to Deb, "Deb, would you mind picking that up? Tuck it away somewhere safe but keep your distance from our friend here."

Deb handed Slasher to me, then walked over and picked up the gun. She did not hold it as I would have —like a large turd about to explode. Instead, she held the gun pointing not at, but toward, the huge, hairy beast, tracing small circles in the air, as if deciding which part of him to blow away.

"Really Sam? My own gun? Planning to leave it behind to confuse the police after you shot me?" she asked.

That shocked him more than Petunia's punch.

He dropped his hands from his still bleeding nose, his mouth dropped open, and he shook his head. He reminded me of a giant cartoon troll who had just been hit over the head by an anvil and was trying to shake it off. A confused look twisted his features.

"What the fuck you talking 'bout?"

Petunia spoke up, "Someone's trying to kill Deb. Now here you are with a gun."

He shook his head. "I heard someone's trying. That's why I'm here."

"To kill her?"

"What? Why would I do that?"

I had to say something. "Well, you certainly didn't look at her with love just now."

He looked around at all of us, confused to the bone. Then he turned to Deb. "Debbie Do?" he almost cried.

Deb sighed. "Now, Sam, you know you shouldn't sneak up on people with guns."

"Wait a minute," I said. "Who is this guy? And what is a Debbie Do? You know him?"

Deb looked a bit embarrassed. "Actually, yes. Meet Sam McElroy, the father of my children. Back then, I was known as Debbie. Debbie Do was his nickname for me."

At this point two police cars pulled up, lights flashing. Evidently the queens who had witnessed the lovers' reunion had stopped screaming long enough to call the police. Two cops popped out of the first car and with minimal conversation, grabbed the man, handcuffed him, threw him into the car, and drove off.

Detective Crawford climbed out of the other car and walked up to us. "You aren't the most popular person around," he said to Deb. "It's going to be a full-time job just sorting out the people who want to kill you. I'm going to take a wild guess here That's the husband?"

"The *ex*-husband," Deb said. "Crawford, I have spent too much time in your company lately. Please do not ask me to come in to make a statement."

"Make a statement?" Crawford asked. "I'm considering putting you in protective custody. It would be cheaper than assigning a detail to follow you around to stop all the exes who are after you."

Deb shook her head. "No detail and don't even think about protective custody. This town doesn't have enough money to pay for how much I'll sue you for if you try. Besides, you know I'm going to win this election. Wouldn't you like to have at least a small chance of winning a single case in my court? Mess with me and I bet I can even get a contempt citation or two stirred up."

Crawford snorted. "I've got plenty of contempt, Ms. Eubank. But that won't stop me from finding out who's trying to kill you. You may not believe it, but I care about what's going on in this town and I don't want anyone—and that includes even you—to have to worry about being blown up or shot. So, I'd appreciate it if you let me do my job."

Deb sighed. "I hate to say it, Crawford, but I'm sorry. I know you are doing your job and I do appreciate it. The thing is that you are wasting your time. Neither of my exes, Sam or Carmen, is responsible for this."

Crawford shook his head. "Says you. Both have the knowledge. Both had the opportunity, as far as I've been able to prove. And from what I know about you, it's not hard to imagine they might possess a desire to blow you into little pieces. The thought has crossed my mind a time or two in the years we've known each other."

"Right back atcha, Crawford. Right back atcha."
"I take it you have nothing to add. You weren't expecting your husband? You weren't planning to meet him here?"

"*Ex*-husband, and this is the first time I've seen Sam in over two years. We prefer to stay in different towns. And no, I hadn't planned to meet him. I don't know why he's here, and I have nothing to add. I do have an important meeting with some of my campaign staff, so if you need to ask me any questions, please give me a call later. Much later. Make it tomorrow or the next day."

"You have a meeting in *Hoosier Daddy*? You're planning a campaign for judge in a gay bar?"

Deb nodded. "Out on the patio. Best nachos in town and I'll be surrounded by friends. So, if there is nothing else " She turned and headed toward the bar.

Crawford shook his head in disgust and headed back to his car.

I hurried after Deb, and Petunia brought up the rear.

Chapter Six
Monday Night at Nacho Mama's Patio Café

Deb seemed unphased by the events in the alley. She stroked Slasher and reassured him that he was the best little butterball in the whole entire world. I, on the other hand, was fighting down the impulse to run screaming into the sunset. I hadn't signed up for this. I had accepted Deb's offer of campaign manager to get a new pair of shoes. Now I had been blown up, used as a decoy in case some crazy was aiming at her, and had almost been witness to or innocent bystanding victim of a shooting by a gun-toting ex. If I was thinking clearly, I would have turned around and run home to hide under the blankets right then. However, clear thinking was not on the day's menu. In addition, I was trapped between two walls of muscle and will—Deb in front and Petunia behind. I allowed myself to be led, feeling a kinship with sacrificial lambs.

Hoosier Daddy was sparsely populated. There was no music in the big back room, so that was empty. The narrow bar at the front held up its usual fossils. Turning right through the doors at the end of the bar, we entered Nacho's domain. A few patrons were out there seeking early evening drinks and munchies. At our usual table, Nacho, Roger, and Foxy KitTan were arguing.

"We have two exes who are in the wind and have the expertise, anger, and inclination to try to take her out," Roger said. "Deb doesn't score high in the 'part as friends' department".

"Ah, but that may be because she is such a catch," Foxy said, gesturing with his cigarette holder. "They may be simply devastated at the prospect of a life without her." Foxy loved the idea of romance. He was superbly wealthy, having founded a chain of perfect pie cafés known throughout the world as *The Pie Hole*. Having sold controlling interest, he was now able to dedicate himself to his amour, Suave, and bringing languid splendor to our corner of the world.

"Once they've tasted Deb, they can't go back to anything bland," Roger said with a nasty leer.

"Once again, dear boy, you have dropped into the gutter," Foxy retorted. "I was speaking of life outside the bedroom. Deborah does possess a magnetic charm and leads an exciting life."

"I don't believe it," Nacho said. "This ain't some lover's beef."

"Or fish," Roger interjected, earning a dirty look from both Nacho and Deb.

"This is bigger than lost romance," Nacho said. "Think about the timing. The husband and the girlfriend have had plenty of time to act before now. This is about the election. We need to keep Deb safe. I want to move her to a house where I can make sure she is protected."

"I have several appropriate properties," Foxy offered. "Suave has progressed from saving pieces of furniture from shops that do not appreciate their beauty to entire houses that might be raped of all their vintage glory. At least it gives us a place to store all the furniture."

"Just a minute, you two," Deb said. "Stop talking about me like I'm not here. I am not about to become a freaking wimp because someone *might* be after me. I've been threatened before."

"Ever had your truck blown up before?" Nacho asked.

"No, but that's not the point. I'm not going to start running and hiding now. There are going to be

threats in the future. If I go all shaky whenever someone looks at me funny, then I might as well quit now. I'll be just as bad as—"

"As BB?" Roger suggested.

I would have protested, but he was right. I was

terrified and had been since the truck had blown up. "I have never pretended to be butch," I said. "Classically elegant, perhaps, but not—"

"Good thing," Roger interrupted. "Your attempt at butchiosity would have been painful for both of us. As for classically elegant, the jury is still out, way, way out on that one."

"Shut up, Roger," Nacho said. "Leave BB alone.

He's not used to all this."

"Used to being blown up? Shot at?" I said, trying to hold back tears. The stress was getting to me. "No, I am not. And I don't have any wish to become used to it. Maybe it is best for everyone if I just leave."

Deb put a firm hand on my shoulder, gripping me so hard it hurt. Of course, that didn't take much.

"No, BB. You can't leave. We have to see this through together."

"She's right, you know, dear boy," Foxy said. "In the unlikely possibility that Nacho is correct and all this trouble is being wrought by some nefarious group and not an ex-lover, they may be concerned that you have some knowledge that could point a finger and in order to clean up loose ends "

I gaped at them with growing horror. "You mean they might want to come after *me*?!"

Nacho nodded. "Sure. That makes sense. You were there at the bombing. You might have seen something. They can't be sure. You're probably safe while they focus on Deb, but after that ... "

"I think I'm going to puke," I said.

"Not out here," Nacho said. "I ain't gonna clean it up. But hold on. What do you mean you were shot at? There ain't been no shooting."

"Coulda been," Petunia said. "We just met Deb's ex-hubbie." She looked at Deb. "You sure know how to pick 'em. After meeting him, I'm not surprised you've sworn off men." She looked back at Nacho. "He had a gun. Now he has a broken nose. Magawatta's finest swooped in and took him away."

Roger grinned. "Only a broken nose, P? You're

getting gentle in your old age."

She shot him a look that would have melted rock. "Make another age crack, bucko, and you'll see how gentle."

Roger ignored her. "So the hubbie is under lock and key. That leaves the latest ex, the girlfriend. You said you don't peg Carmen for it. I'm not so sure. Anyone else?"

"I am quite certain that as a defense attorney, you have been able to anger more than a few people— both defendants you were unable to free and victims of defendants you were," Foxy said. "I fear the number of people who would cherish the idea of damage done to your esteemed self would not be trivial."

Deb nodded. "It's something I got used to a long time ago. That is one of the reasons I have no intention of starting to hide just because someone managed to blow up Boomer, as much as I loved that truck."

"I still think all of you are lookin' in the wrong place. We should be lookin' under rocks and see what crawls out," Nacho said. "There is a very good possibility we are looking at something that goes further than a single person with a grudge. Deb represents something bigger."

"Do tell." Foxy inserted one of his imported cigarettes into his ornate gold and ebony holder. "You make it sound ever so titillating."

Nacho gave a quick look around the patio, ensuring we were away from any prying ears. "I know you got suspicions that I have interests beyond the café."

Few people knew much about Nacho, but I knew a little more – very little more than most. I had actually been drafted to aid in the escape of one of Nacho's Twinks, as they were called, when desperate measures were called for—desperate enough to recruit someone with my skills, or lack thereof. Late one night I was summoned by Nacho. Nothing was explained. Nacho told me what to do and told me in no uncertain terms not to ask questions and to forget everything I saw, was told, and happened. I know how to follow orders and while remembering is sometimes a challenge, forgetting comes quite naturally to me. However, while I was ferrying the fairy, the boy was nervous and a bit talkative. I let him ramble. It seems that Nacho was one of the founders of *TaDah!*—the Twinkie Army Destroying All Hypocrites—a very secret society that monitors and brings down those who publicly rail against and privately roll against pleasures outside the dominate pairing paradigm. While years beyond being of use in the seduction "trenches", Nacho specialized in field command. *TaDah!*'s data gathering equaled some of the world's most notorious debaunchers of privacy, but was only used to defend the personal freedoms so often attacked by gray-lifers who felt no one should be having any fun unless it resulted in profit for their greedy little selves. I instinctively knew better than to ever hint I knew any of this.

No one knew all of Nacho's secrets, and no one was inclined to go poking around beneath Nacho's skirts to find any out. If you come across a dark cave and the entrance is littered with bones and signs are prominently posted that advise, 'Beware' and 'Stay Out', well, even when full of liquid courage or actual stupid, none of us are so dull as to wander in just to find out more details. So, rather than press for more information about these "other interests", we just nodded.

"It isn't generally known, but I have it on good authority that there's about to be a change at the statehouse."

"Another?" Foxy asked. "It was an absolute delight when that white-haired Ken doll was swept away to serve his master's bidding in Washington. I would think that everyone would be keeping an extra low profile since he only escaped being booted by his elevation to a higher arena of sphincter licking."

Nacho nodded. "It seems the lieutenant governor was the dirtier of the two and is about to be surprised by a visit from the feds."

Roger smiled. "Your resources never cease to amaze me, Nacho. Dare one ask how you know about a surprise raid from the FBI?"

Nacho hinted at a rare smile. "Loose lips, Roger. None here. Now, what that means is that the next in line to be governor is the much more liberal Speaker of the Assembly."

"Lovely, I'm sure," Foxy drawled. "However, that hardly seems to have a bearing on our Deborah."

"It doesn't. Except, I also happen to know that one of the more conservative judges on the state supreme court is just about to schedule a weekend getaway of pleasure with a very limber and unconventional young man without the knowledge of the judge's very devoted and very conventional wife. Unfortunately, that weekend is going to end up being the headline of an in-depth and unpleasant exposé of a secret men's club of ill repute. Since that judge is one of the most vocal opponents of any rights for 'them damn queers' as he puts it, I figure he'll be history pretty soon."

Roger smiled. "Nacho now can predict the future."

"Always could, dumpling," Nacho said. "You don't have to be a weatherman and all that. However, that means that the new governor will be looking for a new justice and will be looking for a justice that can make a splash—really make a statement of a new direction for the state."

Even I could follow that. "So, Deb would be a perfect person for that."

Nacho nodded. "Now I got more inside information than most, but there are more than a few groups of right leaning wackos who know the quality of the no class idiots they are keeping in power. They kind of like propping up the morally disabled as long as they know their secrets. Keeps 'em on a short leash and following orders. So, there's been a bit of chatter about the necessity of taking care of Deb, just in case something unpleasant happens to one of their pet politicians. Once our judge got himself in trouble, I wasn't the only one who could see how the dominoes might fall and that chatter rose to a roar. The way I see it, the chances that this is just an angry lover are slim. Very slim. There's too much power in play. For my money, this is about power. It's bigger than Deb."

"And that's saying a lot," Roger said, earning himself a glare from Deb and a solid punch in the shoulder from Petunia. He hardly flinched. I would have lost the use of my arm for a week. "However, I still think we should eliminate the obvious suspects. I agree there may be a conspiracy lurking behind this bush— "

"That's what she said," I interjected, speaking before my brain was fully engaged, then ducked, expecting a barrage of flying objects. When none came, I looked up in time to see multiple eye rolls as attention returned to Roger.

"However, it is still possible the problem is a local one. The police have the hubbie. It may be him. There's your ex, Carmen. Any idea where she is?"

"I'll give you her address. She still works out at the base, so you might find her there during the day."

"I'm not going to look. Can you call her and invite me over?"

Deb shook her head. "It was not the most civil of breakups. I think the final straw was when I called her a lesbrarian."

"Lesbrarian?"

Deb smiled. "She was always checking out women and bringing them home to peruse for a couple of weeks, then she'd return them. She did not find my label amusing."

Roger looked at Petunia. "You up for a little gal hunt?"

"Not for free."

Foxy spoke up, "It would be my pleasure to hire you and Roger and pay whatever it costs to keep our Deborah among the living."

"We really should consider any other locals who may want to take a piece out of Deb," Roger said. "Just to be sure."

"I've pissed off plenty of people over the years. It comes with the territory. I can't think of anyone with the balls to actually do something about it." Deb shrugged.

"Think money," Foxy said. "You'd be surprised how the prospect of losing or gaining a significant amount can make the smallest of balls grow. For many people, particularly men, money and virility are inextricable linked. If Deborah's election may cost or make someone a fortune, that's where you should look."

Deb shook her head. "I mostly do criminal law, and most of those folks have a hard time paying my fee."

I had an idea. "What about that *Save the Swamp* group?"

Roger laughed. "Save the swamp?"

Deb smacked me. "It's *Save the Wetlands*, BB, and they have a point." She explained to the others, "Remember Hamilton Burns, the developer who tore down those classic houses right before historic preservation could declare them protected?"

"Everyone who has rented one of the plastic cells he claims to be apartments calls him BurntHam because he promises something succulent and serves up coals," I said.

Foxy nodded. "Who could forget? I have been unfortunate enough to have to sit at a table with the man. One feels guilty calling him a pig—so unfair to the hog. An aficionado of greed which has nothing to do with the amount in his coffers. He grabs because that is all he knows how to do. It is too obvious he is making up for a lack somewhere else, and I am not even considering the deficit in his morals."

"That's the one. Well, he used a shell corporation to buy one of the last pieces of shoreline at the lake and is planning to pave the whole thing and put in a marina. In one swoop he can destroy the shore, the wetlands, and put so many more boats into the lake, it will probably kill off all the fish. This group is going to sue to stop the project."

Roger nodded. "And who would be the judge to hear that suit?"

"Well, if I win it would probably be me."

"I'll look into it," Roger offered. "I've never liked

the man and I'd love to catch him with his fingers some place nasty. I also wouldn't be surprised."

"Well, if you want to waste your time looking under your noses, go ahead," Nacho grumbled. "But my money is on an outside group. Lots of people with lots of unpleasant resources will do just about anything to keep a lesbian from being in a position to judge anyone. It goes against their limited thinking. *They* do the judging. So, check out what you want, but do it quick."

Deb stood. "It's time for me to get to the Meet the Candidate event. Come on, BB."

"Roger, you go with her," Nacho ordered.

"No," Deb said. "I thought I made that clear. No bodyguards. It sends the wrong message. BB is enough."

"BB is enough for what?" Roger scoffed. "What could he possibly do?"

I agreed completely. If there was any danger, I wanted someone I could clutch in a death grip—well, not actually a death grip, but tightly, very tightly— who would whisk me away to a place of happiness and safety.

"He can hold my briefcase and keep Slasher happy and quiet. Other than that, I don't need anything."

"Just yesterday your truck blew up and—"

"I am aware of that. I am also aware that if people get the idea that supporting me is an invitation to danger, then they won't have anything to do with this election. No one will volunteer to go door to door this weekend. My 'get out the vote' effort will be me and BB. I might as well just give up. So, no security. I'm going to behave like this is a community event at a community center in a little college town in the middle of Indiana, which it is. So investigate away, but keep your distance."

With that, she stood and headed for the door. At the door she turned back and glared at me. "BB, come."

The unknown looming fears were no match for the threat in Deb's eyes. I stood and followed her. At the door, I turned back toward the table. "Help me," I mouthed. Roger didn't move but looked heavenward and made the sign of a cross in benediction.

I made the sign of the bird back at him. "Thanks a

bunch."

"Ah, what are friends for?" he asked.

"I'll let you know when I get some," I said and followed Deb out to her rent-a-car, clutching her briefcase, which she had, of course, forgotten.

Chapter Seven
Meet the Candidates

Magawatta is a small town, so we could have walked. However, the possibility of either local or international psychos gunning for me made me glad we had a car. Yes, I know no one was actually gunning for me, but the chances of being caught by a stray bullet or piece of shrapnel increased in direct proportion to my nearness to Deb, and she was insisting on far too much nearness for me to relax.

"Deb, why do we have to go tonight?" I asked. "You're basically running unopposed and these snoozefests seem to be invented to maximize the pain of attendance. The same group of people attend them all and they aren't going to learn anything new. They stand in line to be able to ask a question they already know the answer to because they somehow believe it makes them look smart, which it doesn't. Then they set about ignoring everyone else who is doing the same thing."

"Oh, BB, you are turning into quite the cynic. This one is just for judge candidates, so the audience will mostly be attorneys and cops who are trying to see what they'll be dealing with. They actually care about the questions and answers. Besides, in a local election, a vote or two can make all the difference. Don't forget, Hawthorne is still on the ballot and is listed as the incumbent. He may be a lecherous old shyster, but he has name recognition. Not many people think about the races for judge before the election. They make up their mind at the last minute. These people in tonight's crowd are some of the few that actually consider who to vote for, so I can't sit back and expect to win. Same goes for

Do a half-assed job and I'll lose. Remember, you get a bonus if I win."

"I think we should consider a bonus for hazard pay no matter how it turns out, now that I'm facing death."

"Ha. Take it up with my accountant." "And who is that?"

"Helen. Helen Wait. Go to Helen Wait."

I was saved from having to come up with an arch reply by our arrival at the Butler Community Center where the evening's entertainment was taking place. Deb grabbed Slasher and I grabbed her briefcase and we headed in. A woman with far too much mascara, a polyester suit, and the unfortunate hairdo of straight bangs contrasting with ringlets piled high atop her head and oozing down her face and neck—which, for some unknown reason, was still popular in Indiana— met us at the door, blocking the way.

"I'm sorry sweetie. No dogs allowed inside."

Deb glared at her. "I am Deborah Eubank, candidate for judge, and this is my service dog. If he doesn't go in, neither do I. Do you want to explain to the crowd that I'm a no show because you refused us entry because you hate animals?"

She paled. "I'm terribly sorry Miss Euba . . . Judge Euba . . . er um, ma'am. I haven't had the pleasure of meeting you before. I'm Lacey Clayborn from Hamilton Burns Properties. I'm helping host this evening's event. Of course, you and your service dog are very welcome. We have a room with refreshments for the candidates to wait in before we introduce you. If you'd come this way."

We followed her into a small room. Deb, conspicuously ignoring the woman, immediately went to study the table of munchies. The lady, having lost any attempt at perky, took the hint and disappeared. I scanned the sad collection of deli platters which looked suspiciously like grocery store specials marked down just before the expiration date. I wasn't about to risk a taste, but Deb was made of sterner stuff. She filled a plate with slices of mystery meat and cheese, sat and began to feed

Slasher and herself, ignoring me and everyone else in the room.

I scoped out the other candidates, trying to evaluate if any of them were capable of a killing spree. They ranged from boring to bored. I recognized most from past events. The few who were in contested races were studiously trying to ignore their opponents while surreptitiously sneaking glances at them. Those who were running unopposed snoozed, played with their phones, or pretended to look busy. No one looked dangerous or interested in taking a whack at Deb, so I relaxed a bit. I worked on convincing myself that nothing could happen in a community center with a room full of lawyers and cops, so the biggest challenge of the evening would be keeping Slasher from peeing on me when Deb handed him off.

A few minutes later, the perky real estate lady came in and ushered all the candidates out to the stage. I followed and took a seat at the back of the room near the door in case Slasher got antsy. The first two candidates were introduced. Each made a short statement and then took questions. The speakers were dull. The questions were even more so. The murmur of the voices and Slasher's soft breathing as he cuddled against my chest lulled me closer and closer to dreamland. A bevy of boys were calling me to join them in a warm pool and I was drifting... drifting.

"We only have one candidate for the superior court position here tonight, Deborah Eubank."

The moderator's voice yanked me back to the forum. Deb walked to the microphone as the crowd politely applauded.

"Thank you all for coming," she said. "I'll keep my remarks brief to allow you more time for questions. The most important thing to know about me is that I am dedicated to—"

BANG. The door to the chamber slammed open and a crowd of people stormed in, led by a short, round, red-faced man with do-wackity crazy eyes, a drunkard's nose, a bad comb over, and a sweat- drenched face. The man carried a large cross in one hand and a bible in the other. He advanced on Deb, theatrically shaking them both at her. I recognized him from press coverage of past demonstrations. It was Harry Felcher, the self-proclaimed pastor of the One True God Tabernacle, a windowless concrete block former auto parts store now charismatic fundamentalist church in nearby Martinsville. He and his minions rarely turned down an opportunity to protest anything that might get their picture in the paper.

"Sodomite! Defamer. Abomination! God will rain down fire upon you. You seek to judge others, but it is you who shall be judged. God will judge you and I, as the servant of the Lord, will strike you down!"

His followers crowded close behind the man, waving signs and crosses while shouting, "Abomination! Repent."

Felcher arrived at the edge of the stage and tried to step up to proclaim on an equal footing and get a shot at the microphone. He got about halfway up. He had one foot on the stage and one on the floor when Deb stepped in front of him. She planted her large, black boot in the middle of his chest and gave him a vicious shove. He fell backward, bouncing off a couple of cops in the front row and landing on his ass, still shouting. His flock screamed and ran toward their fallen idol. Deb stood at the edge of the stage, obviously contemplating a stage dive. When I was young, I enjoyed watching wrestling on TV. It was great theater with obvious good guys and bad guys and scripts that were easy to follow, even for an eleven-year-old. Seeing her perched and ready brought back memories of 'roided muscle men balancing on the top ropes, ready to fly through the air onto a supposedly unsuspecting wrestler who had somehow been completely stunned by falling out of the ring. However, in this case, the action was not staged, and Deb would actually hurt the man. Judging from his flabby body and flushed face, she might even kill him. I'm not a political expert, but I had a suspicion that killing someone, even someone who might deserve it, would not help her campaign. I was not sure what to do. There was no way I was going to try to stop her from the floor. I had no desire to try to catch a boatload of limestone blocks. I had already tried that trick yesterday and still had the bruises to prove how well it had worked for me. The chamber echoed with shouts and screams. I couldn't yell at her to stop. No one's voice would carry over all that noise. I knew I had to do something. Maybe if I got closer, she would see me and Slasher and the piteous look on my face or his would bring her to her senses.

I didn't want to, but I started toward the stage. However, Saint Lance intervened and saved me. Several of the cops, including the two who had been upended when he landed on them, surrounded the irreverent Reverend Felcher, pulled him to his feet, handcuffed him, and escorted him out of the room. His flock of Felcherites followed close behind, screaming about police brutality, muff divers, abominations, and the hell fire that would soon be raining down upon everyone but them.

Even after they left, there was no way for the event to continue. Everyone was out of their seats, chairs were overturned, and no one was interested in sitting back down to a somnambulant Q & A session. The moderator, nonplussed by being forced off script, stammered a few 'under the circumstances' and 'thanks to candidates and voters for coming' type comments and hurried to the back room, obviously in search of a hidden bottle of 80-proof make the world go away elixir.

Deb, a grin splitting her face, hopped off the stage, grabbed Slasher from my hands, and headed toward the door.

“Best event of the entire campaign," she proclaimed. "I must send Harry Felcher a thank you card."

Chapter Eight
The Second Attempt

Deb dropped me at my apartment. I live alone in a small, older house divided into two separate units. It's a bit outside of the student ghetto, but close enough to walk to almost everything and is only a couple of blocks from Beau's house. I get reduced rent for doing small extra tasks around the place—not that any sane person would trust me with power tools, but I can safely take the trash cans to the curb for pickup, shovel the occasional deposits of snow, and be available to let repair people in. The other side of the duplex is usually rented by a grad student. Younger students tend to cluster in one of the newer plastic monstrosities that, like insatiable creatures from another planet, are slowly consuming the town. These complexes rise then fall in popularity within a few years, leaving behind dilapidated hulks. Then the cash fattened developers and elected officials look for new neighborhoods to consume.

I entered my abode, greeted by, well . . . acknowledged by my current feline curators. I don't think anyone owns a cat. The cat takes up residence and allows itself to be provided for. Spot tends to ignore me unless he wants the chair I'm sitting in. Spot is entitled. Any time I lay down, he takes up residence on my chest and occasionally, my head. I like cats. They require little, except food and the occasional cleaning of their box. I would prefer they not express displeasure through barfing, but except for the times that their landmines hide within the pattern of the rug and I take an unexpected step and *squish,* they are little trouble and add a certain amount of calm after a stressful day. I have had live- in boyfriends. I prefer cats. I appreciate quiet when I come home and for a decent interval after I wake up, two times when boyfriends seem most intent on having an "important conversation" about our relationship. While it is acceptable to chase a bothersome cat outside or at least, out of the room, it is frowned upon to do the same with humans.

After a relaxing glass or three of wine and another watching of a well-memorized *South Park* episode—the gods of my idolatry—I was in a much more serene frame of mind. Far more competent and butch people than myself were on the job and I had handled myself with honor—which reminded me it had been a while since I had handled myself, with or without honor—by not running away, fainting, or soiling myself. With these pleasant self- congratulatory thoughts, I drifted to sleep, ready for a long expedition into dreamland.

Alas, it was not to be. The ringing of my phone woke me from a splendid frolic with a man far too young and studly for me, who was ooo'ing over my prowess.

"Mrrphh?" Vocalization upon awakening is not one of my strong suits.

"BB. Deb's. Now." Roger knew that when waking me up, he had to keep things very, very simple. "Don't ask for explanations. Get here now, and I'll explain when I see you."

"Yes, Roger. I'll be right there," I said, hanging up the phone and immediately going back to sleep.

The phone rang again. "Mrrphh?"

"I know you went back to sleep." It was Roger. "I'm going to sing until you are out of bed, standing upright." He immediately launched into it, "Lovin' you ... "

"Stop! I'm awake. I'm awake."

"Are you out of bed?" "Yes," I lied.

"Lovin' you ... "

"Okay, okay! Stop. I'm up. I'm out of bed." Spot was glaring at me from his place at the foot of the bed, having moved off my chest at some point when I stopped petting him. "What's up?"

"As I said, I'll tell you when you get here. Be here in ten minutes. There's no traffic. Do *not* stop for coffee. You are needed. Do *not* make me come and get you."

I sighed. I was awake and, worse than that, I was curious. What could possibly have happened at—I glanced at the clock—three in the morning? As quickly as I could, I pulled on my clothes and headed out to Deb's. I might have been awake, but it was taking a real effort to get my brain to function as I drove. Luckily, there were few drivers on the road. Around campus there were probably several students wandering the roads who had been researching different ways to kill brain cells, but out this way, nearly everyone was deep in dreamland. By the time I got to the short dirt road that led to Deb's place, I was clear enough to face whatever was happening—or so I thought.

Flood lights lit up the yard. All the lights in the house were on. Roger's car was parked near the cabin, right behind Deb's rental car. However, the rental was canted at a weird angle and the side was bashed in. What really caught my attention was the battered truck at the entrance to the yard. This did *not* belong. Both front tires were shredded and long skid marks in the dirt led back to the reason. A spike strip, those things that police throw across the road to end car chases, gleamed in the light. The truck was a wreck. Not just the tires. It had been driven hard and put away wet for a lot of years. The back bumper was held on by rope. Large sections of the body were held together by multiple layers of duct tape. Indiana doesn't require vehicle inspections, so seeing barely held together vehicles driven by barely held together people was not an uncommon sight. But even among the beaters, this one stood out as a true heap. It had the requisite American flag, MAGA, and NRA bumper stickers which held together pieces of the windows.

Tearing my gaze from the truck, I looked up at the house. It had been attacked. The front windows and the glass panel of the front door had been shattered. Looking up to the second floor, I saw the windows of Deb's upstairs bedroom had bullet holes in them.

As a calm and collected adult, I behaved accordingly.

I freaked.

Leaping out of the car, I ran into the house yelling Deb's name. At times like these, my inner fag takes over and for no reason at all, my hands raise to shoulder height and start flapping as if I am trying to fly away on very stubby wings. My vocal cords tighten so my voice raises into the prepubescent and continuously peeps a single word or phrase in a shrill tone. I move quickly in a gait that brings to mind an amalgam of 'runs like a girl'—although, no girl ever did or could run so ineffectively—and mincing. I burst through the shattered door calling Deb's name.

"Jeez, BB, take a pill." Petunia stood in front of an office chair in the middle of the living room, calmly tossing what looked like a small flashlight back and forth between her hands. In the chair, wide- eyed and twitching, was one of Southern Indiana's finest specimens. There is a certain breed or perhaps, inbreed is a better term, that populates the small towns around Magawatta. They often appear in media reports, having been arrested for running a stop sign in front of a cop while smoking a joint on their way to deliver various drugs. They are easily identified by their sunken but piercing eyes, gaunt bodies, neck tattoos, and collections of sores and scabs—a result of their regular ingestion of liquor and meth. I'm not sure if the twitching in this case was the result of additives in his bloodstream or the nearness of Petunia. I'm sure he would have been twitching more, but his hands were tied to the arms of the chair.

"Roger's upstairs with Deb. This pile of crap is Brandon Meeks. Brandon and I are having a little *conversation*." Petunia twirled the flashlight, then reached it out toward the man. He yelped and pulled away as far as the ropes allowed.

I had never seen that reaction to a flashlight. "What is that thing, Petunia?"

"Stun baton. Cute, isn't it? Wanna see what it can do?" She touched an end to the man's arm. He screamed and his arm went stiff, straining against the ropes, then he flopped around uncontrollably. It was painful to watch. I'm guessing it was more painful to experience.

"Petunia!" I protested.

Her face, always hard, became more stone-like. "You can go upstairs, BB, but Brandon and I have some more chatting to do."

This was too much. My legs couldn't hold me up any more. I sank down on a sofa. Petunia turned back to the man, ignoring me.

"Now, Brandon. We can call the cops and have you taken away after we play some more, or you can answer my question. Why did you shoot up this house?"

"I told you! I did it for the money and the dope." The man was crying and shaking. This was no tight-lipped enforcer. He would tell you the pin number of his mother's bank account and steal her ATM card if there was something in it for him. Of course, he was also the type who lied so often he might not be physically capable of telling the truth. However, with Petunia looming above him, threatening him with the baton, he was making a real effort to tell the truth or at least, to seem like he was.

Petunia tapped his head with a finger. "Think, Brandon. You know you want to tell me what I want to know. Here's the big question. Who was going to give you money and dope?"

"I don't know."

Petunia shook her head. "Wrong answer, Brandon." She zapped his stomach and he bucked and screamed.

"I swear! I don't know who it was! You gotta believe me!"

"I don't gotta anything." She considered. "Maybe I should try it on your balls. Might be a favor to the world. Make sure there aren't any more little Meeks spawn running around."

"No!" he begged. "Listen, I can't tell you what I

don't know. This is what happened. I swear. I got a text. The number was blocked. But it told me if I would take out whoever lived here there was $5,000 and an entire ounce of crank in it for me."

Petunia shook her head. "And you just believed a text? Try another one. Even you aren't that stupid. At least, I think you aren't. Am I giving you too much credit?"

"Of course, I didn't believe it. I texted back that I needed some proof. Then I got another text. It said I could pick up a gram and a hundred dollars to prove it was legit."

"Where?"

"The edge of the park they're making at the old depot. There's a dumpster with a burning cross painted on it. Text said it would be right under the cross. I went there and, sure enough, the cash and the crank was there. Good stuff, too."

"And when was this?"

"Last night. So, I planned it for tonight, on acounta I was outta crank, plus that's a lot of money."

Petunia tossed the baton back and forth, looking at him, considering. "I don't know if I should believe you, Brandon."

"It's the God's truth. I swear it on my mother's life."

"I think I'd believe it a little more if I give you another couple of pokes with my new toy."

His eyes bulged even farther out of his head. "No! Please. I tol' you everything I know. Please, lemme go. I'll drive away and never come back and you'll never see me again. I swear. There ain't no amount of nothin' in this world that's worth what you already done to me. Please!"

"P, I think you can let him go." Roger stood on the stairs. "I'd rather not explain how we got the information. I'd also rather not share it just yet."

Petunia still wasn't sure. "Both his front tires are shredded. What do we do with his truck? And him, for that matter. Can't have him walking down the road. He'd get picked up. It's late and he doesn't exactly look like a reputable citizen."

Brandon, sensing the possibility of release, spoke up, "I got a couple of old tires already on their rims in the back of the truck. Them tires I got on it now weren't that good, so I always keep a couple of spares along with a jack. I can be outta here in fifteen minutes if you lemme go."

“Well ..."

"Let him go, P. If you zap him again, he's liable to piss himself and then we'd have to clean it up."

Petunia didn't seem to move, but the baton disappeared and an enormous hunting knife appeared in her hand. Raising it over her head like she was going to perform an old testament sacrifice, she brought it down. Brandon's scream ripped through the air. But he was untouched and the rope on his right hand fell away. With another flick, his left arm was free. Petunia nodded her head at the door, and he scrambled up and out, blubbering oaths that he would never again be seen.

The knife disappeared and Petunia pushed the chair back toward the office. She looked at Roger. "You heard?"

Roger nodded and called up the stairs. "Okay, Deb. It's legal for you to be downstairs."

Deb came down, clutching Slasher and trying to calm his shaking. She walked to a jar of treats and pulled out a few, then sat on the sofa and fed them to him while cooing sweet nothings in his ear. Ah, if only I could have a dog's life one day. Deb’s soft tones calmed Slasher and calmed me, too. We both stopped shaking.

"I was sleeping,” said Deb. “Then I heard a crash in the yard. A few seconds later, a window downstairs shattered. I was in the process of standing up to see what was going on when Roger called and ordered me to drop to the floor." She smiled. "You are probably the only person in the world who can order me to drop to floor when I'm in my bedroom, and I will obey without question. Good thing, too. As I hit the floor, another window exploded downstairs. Then one of the windows up there blew apart and at least three shots went through the other and ended up in the ceiling. If I hadn't been on the floor, I might be singing the blues."

Petunia mumbled something.

Deb looked over at Petunia. "What did you say?" Petunia gave the twitch that passed for her smile.

"That's what she said."

Deb rolled her eyes. "Then, before I could call the police, there was an explosion and a crash in the yard. I heard screams and then a few gravely orders." She nodded toward Petunia. "Sounded like you. That's when I noticed I still had the phone in my hand, and Roger was yelling at me."

Roger grinned. "I was telling you to stay down. I was already on my way."

Deb looked back and forth between Roger and Petunia. "I think I made it very clear that I was to be left alone tonight. It seems you ignored my orders."

Roger smiled and saluted. "And you are very welcome. If you want, I'll make up a story about how Petunia was taking a constitutional and just happened to be walking by your place when—"

Deb sighed. "No. No need. No one, especially me, would believe it and you certainly proved your point. I guess I do need protection. Sam couldn't have done this. He's mad that I divorced him to be with a woman, but he's not this kind of mean. Besides, unless something very odd happened, he's still in jail. Carmen is mad at me and she's hot-tempered. She likes to blow things up, but shooting just isn't her style. Besides, she would do it herself. She'd never hire a washed-up almost man to do anything she cared about. She'd be sure that any man who tried would screw it up, which sounds like what happened."

Petunia grunted. "They'll screw the pooch every time," she shot a glance at Roger, "with occasional exceptions."

"I'll take that as a compliment," Roger said. "Speaking of incompetent men, do you mind if we do not bring Detective Crawford into the mix right away? I feel sure he would insist on putting a protective detail on you and the only thing that will accomplish is to keep us away. Besides, I'm still not convinced he is completely innocent in all this."

"I can't believe . . . well, I won't believe that Crawford would take part. We may not see eye to eye, but—"

"Stop it, Deb. You know Nacho thinks this may be bigger than we originally imagined."

Deb snorted. "Ha. If we were dealing with an international conspiracy, don't you think they could dig up a more competent hit man than that moron?"

"You have a point, but until we know more ... "

She sighed. "Agreed. I'm also fine with not reporting this right now. I don't really relish trying to explain what went on tonight. Speaking of which, what *did* go on tonight? Obviously, you were surveilling. How did you catch him?"

We turned to Petunia. "He wasn't being subtle. Came tearing down the road, swerving from one side to the other. I don't know if he was intending to or if that's the best he could do. I called Roger when I saw him. The dumbass tried doing doughnuts in the yard. I figure he was trying to wake you up so he could get a shot. That's when he ran into your car. I don't think that was planned. He was not what you call a skilled driver to begin with and was pretty obviously impaired. The crash slowed him down a bit. He pulled to a stop outside the house and got out. That's when he did the shooting. I knew Roger had told you to drop to the floor, so I decided it would be more useful to get some intel from him than to take him down. Once he gave up on trying to shoot you and started off toward the road, I threw the spike strip and blew out his tires. The rest you heard."

I had to know. "And how is it you had a spike strip with you? That's a deadly piece of equipment. I thought only police departments had them."

Petunia shrugged. "I never leave home without it. You never know when a situation might arise."

I offered a little prayer that I was never trapped alone with an angry Petunia, which was not an unfamiliar prayer.

"So, what now?" Deb asked.

"Hold on," Roger said, pulling out his phone. "Let me bring Nacho up to speed."

He spoke quickly into the phone. I didn't try to overhear. I did not need more information. My conclusion was that I should be nestled all snug in my bed while visions of hunky men danced in my head. However, I had an unpleasant feeling that I was not going to be enjoying that Christmas fantasy this particular evening. I was right.

Roger hung up and turned back to us. "Nacho wants you to move to a safer place."

Deb shook her head. "No chance."

"We can't protect you here. You are too far out in the country."

"I still don't believe this is some evil plot. I overheard a bit of that story. Did you notice he had no way to collect his money except to send a text? He was obviously not the brightest bulb on the tree, but that is bag of rocks dumb. It sounds more like he and his fellow crackheads got together during a drink- and-smoke-athon and he decided to play scare the dyke. Besides, he's gone and isn't about to try it again."

“Doesn't mean there aren't others who got the same offer."

"If it really was an offer and not a story he cooked up. I think Nacho is being too cautious. Besides, I have client files here. Too many to move. I can't leave them while I have holes instead of windows. I'm out in the woods. There are animals other than humans that might like to wander in and cause a mess. Plus, I'm just not going to be chased away. I've never run before and I'm not going to start now. I can’t."

"But—”

"Stop arguing, Roger. I'm not leaving."

Roger sighed. He hated not getting his way, but he wasn't about to pick up Deb and carry her out. He pulled out his phone again. After a brief conversation, he said, "You win. Nacho is sending someone over with plywood to cover the windows. We'll have the glass replaced in the morning. Petunia will stay outside watching." He looked at me. "BB, you stay inside the house."

"But what can I do?" I protested.

"Raise the alarm. Maybe take the first bullet." Roger grinned. When I paled, he added, "You are mostly here to shoo away any animals that come sniffing around before the plywood gets here and that's already on the way." He turned to Deb. "What's your schedule for tomorrow?"

"In the morning I was planning to catch up on some work. Afternoon, I have three interviews—a magazine, a newspaper and TV." She grinned. "Don't touch that dial, I am going to be a guest on *Wuzzzup Magawatta*."

"I thought that was a morning show," I said. "Filmed in the afternoon, so nobody has to worry about puffy eyes."

Roger considered. "That should work. You stay at home all morning. BB will stay with you. If you need anything, send BB." He shot an evil grin at me. "That way if anyone is planning to ambush you —"

"I have to go to work," I squealed.

"Call in sick."

"But I can't do that, it's lying."

Petunia loomed over me. "What if you told them you had a broken arm? Would that be better?" Her muscles bulged.

A small squeak escaped. "I'll call in sick," I said.

"So, it's decided," Roger said. "Petunia will take you to your interviews." He looked at me. "She's more reliable in a pinch."

A truck pulled up outside.

"Ah, that will be Nacho's friend with the plywood. Fast and efficient. He already had a truck full of plywood for a job. I'll fill him in and then I have things to set in motion. BB, come to *Hoosier Daddy* tomorrow at five and we'll plan next steps." He looked at Deb. "Please, my dear, for once, follow directions and stay here. If you need anything, send BB. P will be your escort tomorrow."

Deb nodded. "Promise. And thank you."

Roger went to the door. He turned and looked at me. "Stay alert. Keep your phone in your hand. P will be here until the sun comes up. If someone gets through P, you'll be the last line of defense, so don't fall asleep." With that, he and Petunia headed outside.

Sleep? I might never be able to sleep again.

Chapter Nine
Tuesday

I did not sleep.

I did not sleep while two of Nacho's compatriots unloaded several sheets of plywood and with butch efficiency, measured, cut, and drilled into place covers for the shattered glass. I did not sleep when Deb, yawning and surprisingly unperturbed, took Slasher out to do his doggie duty. I heard Slasher start barking and I was up and to the door before more sensible thoughts about taking cover or hiding were able to control my motor functions. Happily, Slasher was just barking at Petunia, who faded out of the shadows near the edge of the yard and held a finger to her lips. Slasher immediately fell silent and went about his business. He trotted back and hopped up the steps. Deb gave him a treat, then scooped him up and headed upstairs.

"Goodnight, BB. I'll wake you in the morning."

"I'll be up."

She snorted. "Yea, right."

She went upstairs and after a few minutes, her snores rumbled through the house. I did not sleep.

The minutes ticked by. I held my phone at the ready and listened for any sound that foretold of an impending attack by the hordes of baddies I was certain were lurking outside. I could sense the army of evil-doers that was at this moment overpowering Petunia. It would take an army, but I was positive they had one.

I did not sleep.

When Slasher leapt onto my chest and began to enthusiastically lick my face, I jolted awake. I sat up, "What happened?" I asked. Waking for me is not a sprint, but a slow toddle. I fear what it will be like in my dotage. "I couldn't sleep."

"You could. You did. You fell asleep," Deb answered. "Despite that, no one else tried to kill me last night. Nacho just called. The window folks are on their way. I've got work to do, so make yourself at home. Why don't you keep Slasher? He likes you and he slows me down in the office."

The morning passed quickly. I engaged in deep conversation with Slasher and we both napped while windows were installed and legal work was done by those best suited for the tasks. All was right with the world when Deb woke me up again by picking Slasher off my chest, where he was busy keeping me from floating away.

"I'm off to my interviews," she said. "Petunia will be guarding my body. You actually have some time off. Try to spend it productively."

I saluted and she headed off. "Lock the door when you leave," she called back. "Arm the security system and make sure you lock the deadbolts on both the front and back doors."

I headed to the kitchen for a little nosh. On the counter was her briefcase—forgotten yet again. I grabbed it and ran after her, swinging it above my head. Petunia was just heading out of the yard but saw me and drove back. Panting, I handed the briefcase to Deb. "I wish you would give up on the damn case," I said. "It's too heavy and you never remember it. I carry it more than you do."

"It comes in handy," she replied. "Besides, it gives you some exercise. Thanks."

They left and I returned to the house, locked everything securely, armed the alarm, and went home for a long bath and exfoliation before a foray into the stack of "must reads" that were growing by my bed. If I was a dedicated employee, I could have gone in and listened to Dustyn sample his latest whine. However, I had already called in sick and I could not see any reason to ruin a perfectly calm afternoon. I needed it. I deserved it.

That evening around five, I headed off to *Hoosier*

Daddy. Picking up a drink at the long bar in the front, I headed out to *Nacho Mama's Patio Café.* Around our usual table, most of the usual suspects were gathered. Beau raised his glass to me, then motioned toward his Aunt May, who was in the midst of one of her reminisces. Aunt May always shared whatever popped into her head, which was usually carnal. She was adored by us all.

"It puts me in mind of Permillia Butterworth," she said as I sat down. "Permillia was the biggest fornicatress in Honeysuckle Springs, and that was saying something. Why, next to her, I was practically a nun. Her sister actually was a nun—Sister Hortense Bottomly, of the order of St. Hortense, the patron saint of fallen women. However, Permillia was no nun. She was reputed to have a forked tongue or at least the talent of one. The muscle control in her privates was so that she had been known to hold a man captive both figuratively and literally for hours. We tried to be polite, but there was always a touch of envy when her name came up. Once a man had been with Permillia, none of the other girls stood a chance. That man was hers for the taking, whenever she wished for as long as she wished. Thankfully, she was primarily interested in quantity. Once she had bedded a man, she had no use for him and would chase him away if he hung around. She used words at first, but she had no compunction about using buckshot, and she was both fast and accurate with a gun. She proved that on more than one occasion. Permillia never took a nickle for her activities and died quite penniless, having never married, of course, and run through her inheritance. Her sister absolutely refused to allow her to be buried in consecrated ground, which I felt was rather spiteful. However, the older gentlemen in town took up a collection and mounted a lovely stone for her in the non-sectarian section of the town cemetery."

Aunt May took a sip of her drink. "And every year, on the anniversary of her death, someone leaves a lovely arrangement of tulips on her grave. No one has ever discovered who."

Aunt May sighed and sipped her drink again. "It

does seem appropriate to gift her with tulips as Permillia was so generous with hers."

"Artistry should be saluted in kind," Foxy KitTan proclaimed. "I hope no one tried too hard to discover the bestower of flowers. It seems appropriate that the homage remain a private affair, as that is what it salutes." Foxy was not a regular to our table, but always came to Tia's *Parade of Gowns* drag show on Sunday evening. He spent most of the rest of his time overseeing his household, holdings and his beloved Suave. I wondered what he was doing here but was not about to ask. This was Nacho's show, with Roger playing the second lead, and I had already been pulled into more danger than I wanted just as a bystander.

Roger grinned at me. "I see you fought off all intruders, BB."

"No thanks to you. No one else showed up or if they did, Petunia took care of them. I didn't ask. I didn't want to know. I also do not appreciate you leaving me in such a precarious position. I do not have a wish to die young, in case I hadn't mentioned that over the years."

"BB, it's been years since you coulda died young," Nacho said, clumping up, leaning on the ever-present cane, noxious cigar anointing all with gut wrenching fumes. "And you never had a shot at leaving a pretty corpse. But I ain't got time for that. We gotta figure what to do to keep Deb alive, despite the fact she refuses to act smart."

"What's the news from your sources?" Roger asked.

Nacho pulled out a chair and sat. "Looks like my first instinct was wrong. By all accounts, this *is* a local matter. Last night's idiot dance convinces me of two things. First, no national group would hire such a fuckup to do their dirty work. That's in line with what my sources report. No one has heard of any action from any of the national prick groups. Interest, yes. Action, no."

"But what about the bomb?" Roger asked. "That wasn't any speed freak pipe bomb. That was constructed by someone who knows what they're doing."

"That brings me to my second observation," Nacho said. "This ain't the work of a single person. Someone with contacts to a variety of shady individuals is trying to hire someone to take out Deb."

"From what I have heard of the ex-husband," Foxy stated, "he is a lone wolf with hardly two nickels to rub together. While he might wish varied manner of unpleasantness to befall our Deborah, he does not seem to have the temperament or resources to lead such a conspiracy."

"You got that right," Nacho said. "I had him checked out. He hates her for, as he puts it, 'lezin out,' but he also often and loudly proclaims his honor as a defender of womanhood. My source in the police says that since they busted him, he keeps insisting that he came to town to protect her once he heard someone tried to blow her up. Plus, he's as dumb as an old turd. Everything I've heard backs that up, crazy as it sounds."

"You have sources in the police department?" I asked.

Nacho didn't answer; instead I received a glare that nearly snapped my spine. I let the matter drop.

"Carmen is also out," Roger said. "She has the knowledge to build the bomb, but she's a lone wolf. She wouldn't hire anyone else to do her dirty work, and she wouldn't hire herself out for do the dirty for anyone. Plus, she hates speed and anyone who has anything to do with it. Her sister was killed in a car crash because of a tweaking driver and her cousin OD'd. Plus I did a little checking and she's very occupied with a new lady. From all reports, she spends every free minute in bed."

Nacho nodded. "I got the same info. So that means we got a mystery someone who is plenty mean but isn't very good at directing a conspiracy, and has an unknown potential pile of killers. At least that's what it looks like to me. Anyone disagree?"

We looked at each other. Roger said, "So who is the spider weaving the web?"

"That preacher was definitely calling down the wrath of heaven last night," I said. "His followers fit the profile of not-so-bright and willing to do just about anything for money and/or speed. I don't know if any of them are smart enough to make a bomb. Maybe someone could look into it."

"I've met people like that from back home," Beau said. "Lots of them know about making bombs. The holy trinity—guns, bombs and Jesus, with a side helping of general bigotry."

"I can look into it," Roger said.

"I picked up a bit of gossip at the last Chamber luncheon which may be relevant," Foxy offered.

"You go to Chamber of Commerce luncheons?" Roger asked, raising an eyebrow. "I can't imagine why."

Foxy smiled and waved his cigarette holder. "I am, of course, a member, as *The Pie Hole* is larger than nearly all other businesses in town. I attend because it amuses me to add a bit of diversity to the gatherings. I enjoy seeing the racist homophobes attempt to smile when they see my rich, gay, black ass saunter through the door. Of course, there are a few interesting members and we enjoy stirring the pot, as it were."

Roger nodded. "I can see the appeal."

"Lovely story," Nacho grumbled. "Is there a point to it?"

"Apologies," Foxy said. "During a lull in the conversation, one of my fellow diners mentioned that our least favorite land developer, Hamilton Burns, aka BurntHam, is planning a new monstrosity. He has evidently bought up a sizable number of lakeside cabins on the QT and is planning to announce a new private boat club and condo development on Lake Magawatta. All very exclusive, pretentious and, I am certain, ugly, as that is his specialty."

"It's the thing the *Save the Swamp* people were protesting," I said. "But that's a lot bigger than they were talking about. They only knew about a couple of lots that he wants to turn into a marina. That's bad enough, but if he gets his hands on the land those cabins sit on, it's going to be huge."

"He can't do that," Beau protested. "No one can

build anything on the lake. The few cabins that exist are grandfathered in, but putting in a new development . . . there's no way he can do that without—"

"Without dealing with several lawsuits," Foxy finished with a smile.

Roger matched Foxy's smile. "And those lawsuits will end up before the new judge and if that is Deb—"

"She hates crappy developments in general, and she hates BurntHam in particular," Beau finished.

"He definitely has the connections to sullied individuals and the ethical insufficiency to be our mystery man," Foxy said.

"You're right," Nacho grunted. "Someone'll have to look into it."

"Perhaps you might also consider," Aunt May started, examining her glass before taking a sip, "the danger of a decapitated snake."

We stared at the little lady, wondering if she had, at last, found the amount of liquor that caused intoxication.

She smiled at us. "Reptiles have slow metabolisms. It takes a while for the message to travel to the brain. There have been cases where the head of a snake has bitten an unwary victim up to an hour after it had been completely severed from the body."

As a dedicated collector of trivia, I joyfully filed this tidbit away without seeing how it was at all useful to our present situation. However, Nacho's eyes gleamed and an appreciative smile flashed by quickly. "You ain't no ditsy broad, May. You're thinkin' that maybe "

"He *is* still on the ballot, is he not?"

"What are you talking about?" Beau asked.

"Your aunt is suggesting that Judge Hawthorne may still want to be in the running," Roger explained. "The man is both clever and sneaky. I knew he was sneaky but hadn't suspected he could be clever."

"After those pictures with the coach's sons?" I protested. "Leather-clad and shackled is not a good look for a judge. He can't possibly think he has a chance of winning."

"He can if he's the only live person running," Roger said.

Beau and I finally made the connection. Beau's mouth formed a shape better suited to a hustler about to get to work. Realizing the unseemly picture he presented, I quickly brought my lips together and attempted a wise nod. "And with Deb out of the picture, he would win."

Roger rolled his eyes. "Welcome to the conversation, BB." He turned to Nacho. "So, we have three potentials. What do we do about it?"

"Protection has to be our first priority," Nacho said. "The election is next Tuesday. If Deb is still alive when polls open, everything changes. It's a whole lot more serious to take a shot at an elected official instead of some uppity dyke."

"Maybe she should drop out," Beau said. "That way they get what want, but she stays safe."

I shook my head. "Have you ever had an argument with her? The more you push, the harder she pushes back. Even if she started this campaign just to stir up the old poop heads, after being threatened, Deb will swim through lava before she'll drop out." I looked at Nacho and Roger. "She also isn't going to hide, slow down her appearances, or accept protection. I, on the other hand, would love to do all three."

"Ain't gonna happen, cream puff," said Nacho. "You're the best card we've got. She'll let you stick around and if someone takes a shot, there's always the chance your broad butt will get in the way."

"That is wonderfully reassuring. Glad to know you care."

Nacho grunted. "You'll live. They're after Deb, not you. The friends I got coming in from out of town can handle protection. Deb doesn't know them, so she won't notice them and kick up a fuss."

"Can they blend into a crowd?" I asked. I strained to imagine what Nacho's associates might look like. Nacho was not a person who could be overlooked by anyone more aware than the dead or comatose. Always attired in a muumuu, combat boots, one brightly colored kerchief at the throat and another around the head, occasionally topped with a chef's hat, Nacho stood out.

Nacho glared at me. "They are young, sweet and innocent looking, but dangerous. So, if you see anyone new to town who is clearly out of your league, don't mess with them, BB, because if they don't hurt you, I will."

"Will they be here in time for my fundraising party for Deborah tomorrow night?" Foxy asked.

"No worries. I'll make sure they are in place." "What about tonight?" I asked. "Deb is scheduled to be at the Get Out the Vote rally. It's on the square. No way to protect her there."

We all considered. The rally was going to have a large crowd in a very public place with a number of clear sight lines from buildings that ringed the square. Plus, Deb would be up on a stage, raised above the crowd, which would make it easier for any evil-doer to spot her and do whatever evil the evil- doer did.

Beau brought down his drink with a bang. "Tia!" he exclaimed.

I looked around. "Where?"

TiaRa del Fuego was a dear friend and the emprasaria of the *Parade of Gowns* drag show at *Hoosier Daddy* every Sunday evening and a beginner's night on Wednesday. Tia was the biggest star in our little world and a performer of strangely unique abilities. However, she rarely ventured out on evenings she was not performing. Seeing her on a Tuesday, particularly this early on a Tuesday, would be cause for at least interest and perhaps alarm.

"No, not here," Beau said. "Tia will have a solution." When Beau was struck by an idea powerful enough to break through his usual haze, there was no stopping him. He pulled out his phone, dialed, and was soon engrossed in conversation with our sorceress of song. He disconnected and picked up his drink in triumph. "Taken care of." He beamed. "TiaRa will call some friends and all the girls will get dolled up and will appear with Deb en masse, dressed in judge's robes. It will be a parade of judges. They'll be shaking and dancing all around, so no one will be able to single her out."

“Wait," I said. "I don't doubt that Tia can pull a gaggle of drag queens out of her wig, but how will she costume them in robes?"

Beau smiled triumphantly. "One of her admirers runs the laundry that has the court account. She checked and she has access to as many robes as we need. And to make things perfect, if there are any unfortunate accidents with makeup or drinks, the robes can be cleaned before they are returned."

Yet again, Beau's inspiration led us across the abyss of the impossible. I had to salute his achievement in his preferred way. I ordered him a new drink.

Roger spoke up, "So that's protection. What about getting at the spider that's spinning the web? We need to figure out who is doing this. If we can stop them, then the problem is solved."

“Why don't you look into the developer?" Nacho suggested. "I already have some work done on Judge Hawthorne."

Roger raised an eyebrow. "I don't suppose you knew ahead of time when, what, and where the coach's sons were planning to—" A hard look from Nacho stopped his question. I wish I had that power.

Aunt May's dulcet tones broke the silence. "Perhaps I might be of some help with the preacher and his followers." Aunt May patted her lips with a lace handkerchief. "I have had some success with men torn between rapture and pleasures of the flesh. Why, I recall one July when a traveling preacher brought his tent revival to Honeysuckle Springs for an entire weekend. It was as hot and humid as only a Louisiana summer day can be. I had been pursuing Harland Fitzwilliams for quite a little while, but he had his eyes on the Lord and had resisted every single one of my advances up to that point. However, I continued my efforts, as he was a most attractive young man and I had an intuition that his will was weakening. That preacher arrived on a Saturday and held forth from just after supper to well past midnight. One might have anticipated some respite from the heat once the sun set, but it was not to be. Not the slightest breeze stirred that hot, thick air. And inside that tent, with all those people, clapping and praising the Lord—of course, I did not attend, but you could hear them from anywhere in town— well, that tent must have rivaled Hell's own climate. People were falling like autumn leaves and being carried out. So many had succumbed, there might have been more outside the tent than there were in. But that preacher kept right on preaching and calling down the Lord and Harland was rooted in front of him, staring up at that preacher like he was standing in front of the Almighty himself. Then, I am told, Harland's head flew back, and he let go a scream that rose up to Heaven and then that boy fell down on the ground, thrashing about and speaking in tongues.

A group went to take him outside, but before they could reach him, Harland jumped up, yelled, 'I have been commanded by Jesus Christ himself and I know what I must do.' He ran right out of that tent and down the main street, tearing off his clothes as he went. By the time he reached my house, he was naked as the day he was born, with a glorious erection leading the way. He threw open my door and shouted, 'May, I have come to bless you with my sacred seed!' I was taken aback, but for only a moment, for this was a prize I had been seeking. I have never been one to look a gift horse in the mouth."

Aunt May took a small sip of her drink, looking back to the scene. "Gift horse was a proper term for Harland, for he was generously endowed in both length and girth. Additionally, he was delightfully indefatigable. He was able to perform splendidly until dawn. Quite sated, we fell asleep in each other's arms. When I awoke, he was gone, never to be seen again. I heard conflicting stories. Some say he returned to the revival, was saved and thereafter, dedicated himself to the Lord. However, I heard from a friend who traveled to New York City that he had become a stud for hire among the highest of high society." She took another sip. "I hope for the benefit of women everywhere that the second story is correct. But I was suggesting that I lend my hand to investigating this had become a stud for hire among the highest of high society." She took another sip. "I hope for the benefit of women everywhere that the second story is correct. But I was suggesting that I lend my hand to investigating this local preacher and his flock."

"That's a good idea," Roger said. "They clearly are not all that bright, but even they should be able to tell that we're all queer. That would horrify them beyond speech, so we wouldn't be able to get any useful intel. BB and Beau couldn't pull off going undercover. I won't do it. And Nacho, with all due respect, you exude a certain unique personality that even the dullest of his sycophants would identify as not cut from the same cloth as them."

Nacho nodded. "Got that right. Aunt May, can you handle the whole bunch?"

"I am not as young and supple as I once was, so I intend to use more inquisition than proposition. That being said, I believe I will be able to ingratiate myself."

"You be careful, Aunt May," Beau warned. "I don't want to have to rescue you from the clutches of those wackos."

She patted his cheek. "My dear, Beauregard, I promise that I shall take my time and use every caution. I do not expect any trouble, but if anything should arise, I hope you will not be offended if I contact Roger instead of you, as I fear you are less equipped to ride to the rescue."

"Got that right," Roger said. "I'd rather have a senile shih tzu as a protector. Beau, you are many things, but a defender of virtue, be it yours or anyone else's, you are not."

Beau considered a retort, but faced with an essential truth, decided that deflection was a better course of action. He ordered another round, then looked toward the doors that led from the patio into the confines of *Hoosier Daddy*. "Here comes the candidate now. I suppose our little confab is over."

I looked up and saw Deb coming toward us, Slasher clutched to her chest. Petunia followed close behind. I couldn't tell if the scowl on Petunia's face was the result of something that had happened or was her usual method of greeting. I wasn't about to ask.

Chapter Ten
Tuesday Night

Deb knew she had been the subject of our conversation—the sudden silence proclaimed it. However, the offer of a drink and multiple expressions of deep interest in campaign updates diverted her attention for the moment. The interviews had gone well, except for Petunia slightly injuring an assistant producer who rushed onto the television set a bit too quickly in order to adjust a light. The incident might have resulted in more serious consequences, but it turned out the man had recently moved to Indiana and had left behind his regular dominatrix. So when Petunia bent his arm and forced him to his knees, he was more inclined to pursue than prosecute.

Deb knew we were up to something but was unable to dislodge any information. She focused her questions on me as the obvious weakest link, but fear of reprisals from Nacho and Roger kept me from blabbing. I was proud of myself, but honestly, had to attribute my accomplishment more to her being tired from the interviews than my ability to resist her interrogation. Nacho clumped off to whip up some food for the table and make sure all was well in the kitchen. Roger kept a firm hold of the conversation, intervening whenever Deb attempted to find out what we had been discussing. However, with both Beau and me notoriously unable to keep secrets and Deb's skill in digging information out of the most resistant witnesses, I had no doubt that she was just biding her time and gathering her strength. We all knew that soon the table discussion would be over, and she would be able to get me alone and my chances for keeping my mouth closed were between slim and none. I looked across at Beau. He was about to explode. He knew something that mattered and Deb didn't, and he couldn't stand it. Despite Roger's deadly glares, he was going to pop in three . . . two . . . one . . . .

"Tia's going to meet us at the rally tonight!" he said, breaking into Roger's detailed description of a boy he initiated into a whole new experience of manhood at a frat party he had recently crashed. Roger had a special love of seducing young men who were aggressively hetro. He never used deception or drugs of any kind, merely divine indifference. "It's a service I provide to help them get in touch with a broader view of humanity," he would say with a smile. However, his story was left unfinished as Beau's outburst turned Deb's newly wakened attention to him.

"Why would she do that?" she asked. "Tia is not one for crowds outside her shows."

Beau looked like a small child who had been found with a marker in hand next to a crude drawing on a wall. He was obviously digging deep to unearth either an excuse to explain away his outburst or an alternative tidbit to captivate the conversation and turn away the attention he had, up until moments before, so desperately sought. However, Beau was not a quick thinker and did not possess either imagination or guile enough to invent an alternative reality. He looked around for help.

And the universe provided. Nacho picked that moment to reappear with platters in hand. Heaps of the wonderful nachos which all Magawatta loved, as well as an assortment of other delicacies, pulled our attention from Deb's question to the promise of gluttonous pleasure. However, the break was a respite, not a deliverance. After a proper span of inhaling delights, Deb again turned to Beau.

"Beau, you were speaking of Tia. Explain. Don't make me force you. You know I can . . . and it might hurt."

Beau looked at Nacho, pleading for help.

"We still don't know if there are more shitbirds

out there," Nacho stated. "You need some protection."

Deb shook her head. “I've told you. No bodyguards. It will send the wrong signal. Besides, what can TiaRa do? She sings wonderfully. She can line up a great show. However, a long, thin drag queen, as regal as she may be, cannot do much against an attack of anything but the blues."

"We know you won't allow protection," Nacho replied. "Wouldn't work in such a public place at night anyway. So, we've asked Tia to provide cover."

“Cover?"

“Congratulations," Roger said. "You are the newest member of the Dancing Judges, a troupe of drag performers, plus one real judge-to-be."

“You'll be a big hit," Nacho said. "And with all the other robes flying, no one will be able to get a clear shot."

"I don't know," Deb murmured.

"Please, Deb," Beau said. "I have never been one for politics, but if just once I can see a chorus line of drag judges dancing in the town square, I will forever know my life has been worth living."

Deb looked around the table and sighed. "If I don't say yes, you are going to do something sneaky, am I right?"

"You can bet your combat boots," Roger replied. "Then I might as well," Deb said. "Better the drag queen you know"

"Thank you," I said. I knew I was going to be on stage or near the stage, and I didn't want to be the only alternative that might get in the way of whatever mayhem arose.

"And here is our lady now," Beau said. At the door to the patio stood TiaRa del Fuego. At night in *Hoosier Daddy*, she was a star, but even in the early evening, dressed down in a Proenza Schouler knock- off, hiding behind large dark glasses, Tia grabbed your eye and held it. This was a personage, floating a bit above the mere mortals. Removed from us, not by foisting an attitude, but because she was focused on a different star than the rest of us. However, she did occasionally descend to bless us with a song or an event, for she was a beneficent deity, if a bit on the spacey side.

She floated toward our table, removing her shades, showing the excitement lurking in her eyes. "All is in readiness," she announced. "I was able to impose upon the owners to use the dressing rooms here to assemble the volunteers. We shall have a bit of a run through in the show room as at this time of the evening, it is empty. Deb, dear, will you take part?"

Deb's face got red and she opened her mouth to explain exactly what she thought about the whole idea. However, TiaRa leaned forward and touched a finger to Deb's lips.

"Of course, you are too busy to engage in such raucous behavior. We shall draft someone to represent you during our rehearsal. I am sure you will be perfection. How could you be anything but? When the performance begins, simply ignore us as we weave about, conjuring a distraction. Hmmm, who is willing to play Deb for now? It only requires that you stand silent and erect and slowly walk forward. Perhaps Beauregard? Have you the wherewithal to be a stand in?"

"I don't know if he can be either silent or erect," Roger said. "His specialties are babbling and erectile dysfunction, from what I've heard."

"Hush, Roger," Tia scolded. "There is no reason to be mean-spirited or tawdry. Beauregard will do a wonderful job. Perhaps you can put yourself to better use by using the muscles in your arms and back instead of your jaw. My friend's van must be here by now, brimming with robes and other accouterments of judicial finery and a touch of elegance. He said he would park in the alley. Do be a dear and pop out on a mission of retrieval, yes?"

Tia lay a comforting hand on Deb's shoulder. "Allow me to do this for you, Your Honor. It will set many minds at ease and erase the possibility of being forced to engage in a horrific contemplation of what- if."

Deb looked up at TiaRa, who returned her gaze with a dreamy smile. She considered Tia's words, then gave a tight nod. "You are right, Tia. This may be bigger than me. Please stay out of my way when I'm on the stage but do as you think is best."

Tia nodded, then drifted away, Roger and Beau in her wake. TiaRa was able to corral a bevy of boys in counterfeit busts full of dreams, trauma, and glamour twice a week to stage a wonderful show at *Hoosier Daddy* despite melodramas and meltdowns. She had just demonstrated how she managed to pull off such a feat.

Deb stood. "Thanks for the eats, Nacho. Come on, BB, let's walk over to the square. They told all the candidates to get there early."

We started away from the table. At the door, she turned back and looked at Petunia. "You're going to follow me, aren't you? Even if I tell you not to."

Petunia shrugged. "You want me to answer that?"

Deb smiled. "Come on. It might be easier to watch out for me if you aren't also having to hide from me."

Petunia nodded and followed us out through the bar and into the growing dark of a late October evening in our little Indiana college town.

Chapter Eleven
Get Out the Vote Rally

The town square was only a few blocks away from *Hoosier Daddy*. Deb set a fast pace, as usual. Petunia followed about a half a block behind. Within minutes, I was trying to keep up, panting and lugging that stupid briefcase.

"Deb! Would you please slow down a bit? We're early, remember?"

"Jeez, BB. You're in terrible shape. If a little bit of walking wears you down, what's going to happen when you get old?"

"When I am old, I shall wear my trousers rolled, eat a peach, avoid the beach, and I shall either totter or sit in a chair pushed by a young stud. I gave up on being butch when I was totally humiliated in junior high gym class," I gasped.

Deb slowed a bit. "Come on, Mr. Muscle. We're almost there."

The square was already busy. Overhead lights had been strung from the buildings that lined the square to encourage shoppers to begin ringing in the holiday season despite it only being the end of October. The major holidays in Magawatta are the ends of each semester, Halloween, and desperate attempts to get students in a Christmas mood early. Magawatta easily lost a third of its population when the students left, so businesses attempted to start the Christmas season earlier every year. Soon I suspect Santas will be greeting students when they move into dorms at the beginning of the semester in September. However, it made the Get Out the Vote rally that much more festive.

Politics in Magawatta is peculiar. Indiana is a solidly red state, except when it isn't. At the Northern end, there is some hope of civilization. Nestled deep in the much more rural and conservative Southern end of the state, Magawatta is a severe cultural oasis, a bit of blue in a sea of red. As gerrymandered districts mean that a single, liberal representative from the area will be forever silenced by the overwhelming majority of troglodytes in the state assembly, the lefties in town take out their frustrations in odd, sometimes amusing, sometimes troubling ways. Primary elections are often bitterly fought with rivals accusing each other of being sycophantic stooges of the middle or even, *gasp,* the right. Council meetings are graced with endless arguments between those who smell a reactionary behind every motion. The local farmer's market is regularly picketed by those who wish to do background checks on all vendors to ensure none are less than good ol' hippy folk. The problem the local Dems routinely face in the general election is that, tired by the fights of the primary election and either delighted that the proper glorious defender of good had won or sulking because the election had of course been rigged, people tend to forget to vote. The turnout is routinely extremely low. In many races this doesn't matter, because the Republican party in Magawatta is a worn and tattered thing. Pictures of their conventions provide a warm glow in my heart, seeing the few, the unhappy few, the band of idiots. So, the Dems routinely win local races. The state is hardcore red, so the turnout for races at the top of the ballot is for the personal sense of civic duty or pride. However, for the occasional local races that actually have a contender, the turnout is often so low there is a chance of losing. Judges in particular seemed to swing to the right and stay, as had happened for years in the case of Judge Hawthorne. So, getting out the vote was important for Deb.

To drum up support, the Dems had gone all out on this rally. A stage was set up on the lawn and several musical offerings were being slopped all over everyone who could not avoid listening—from a painfully loud thrash band, to a couple of singer/songwriters of the meaningful wail variety, to a spoken word "edgy" poet. A local DJ MC'ed the whole mess, throwing in purportedly interesting and insightful comments, plus the occasional rap attempt and audience participation fail. Food trucks ringed the square, so there was plenty to munch. Flyers touting various causes were being handed out and immediately tossed on the ground. A few joints were being passed. There were even torches flaming at the corners of the stage. It would have been festive and enjoyable had I been several years younger, not carrying a heavy briefcase and not busy praying that some psycho was not plotting to kill Deb with me as an addition—either by accident or for good measure.

Deb slowed and waded through the crowd, greeting all she knew and exchanging a few words here and there. This was, after all, the reason for such events. While I am happy sequestered at home with cats and media, Deb actually enjoyed being around people and talking with them. Ah, well, there's a customer for every dress. We made it to the backstage area. The event was well-organized, with clear instructions of where to go and what to do and when to do it.

Deb handed Slasher off to me and mixed with the supporters backstage. I found a chair and dozed, briefcase beside me and Slasher cuddled to my chest. I suppose I should have been looking for suspicious characters making suspicious movements, but I doubt I would know a suspicious movement if it bit me in the ass, so I did what I do best—I thought happy thoughts and tried to ignore the world.

Between acts that were supposed to keep the crowd interested, candidates made speeches and organizers encouraged people to sign up to walk the precincts that weekend and to bring out the vote on election day. Someone bumped my shoulder, startling me awake.

"Atta way to keep a look out," Roger said, grinning down at me.

I shrugged. "I haven't seen anyone who looked dangerous."

"You haven't seen anything but the inside of your eyelids," he said. "Pay attention. Deb's about to be introduced."

I stood, moving so I could see the stage. At the microphone, the head of the local Dems was creaming her jeans about the real opportunity to get rid of one of the old guard conservative judges who held the court in their grip for too long. The sordid scene at the motel that lay at the core of Deb's chances was not mentioned. It didn't have to be. Everywhere in the crowd, people were nudging each other and grinning as they recounted the story that had delighted all. I even saw a few pantomimed reenactments. Beside me, Roger tensed. He also was scanning the crowd, but not for amusement.

From the stage, the woman cheered, "And now, I'd like to bring out our next judge . . . Deborah Eubank!" Deb, robe bedecked, began to walk toward the mic.

Those in the crowd who were paying attention clapped. It was less than tumultuous. Judicial races weren't exactly cutting-edge entertainment. I had a brief thought that actual judge racing, with candidates in robes, jumping hurdles and perhaps dodging obstacles and booby traps, would certainly stir up more excitement. But then . . ..

From the street along the edge of the crowd, two enormous RVs with flashing strobe lights on top and multicolored chasing lights tracing racing stripes down each side, turned and jumped the curb, blasting air horns to split the crowd, heading for the stage. I gasped in horror, not sure whether to run away or move to protect Deb.

I looked at Roger. His face lit up with a wide grin. "Foxy told me he had arranged for an extra surprise," he said.

I looked back at the RVs, much closer now and recognized the pink and black logo of Foxy's chain of eateries emblazoned on the sides. A loudspeaker blared, "Make way for the *Pie Hole*. Pie coming through. Make way for the *Pie Hole*. Plenty for everyone!"

The RVs made it almost to the stage and came to a stop, music blaring, their lights turning the event into an outdoor disco. The doors of each one flew open and from inside, a plethora of judges poured out into the square, but judges like the world has never seen. Enormous wigs reached to the sky. Bosoms of unbelievable girth and perkiness jutted out like the prows of a mighty armada. The robes – barely fastened – revealed gams to make Grable grovel with envy. And they were dancing and whooping and kicking and prancing. They poured onto the stage and formed a bobbing, weaving bevy of arms and wigs and bodies that shimmied around Deb. She did her best to ignore the churning mass and spoke directly to the suddenly excited crowd as if she was speaking personally to each one of them. They screamed and roared. She played them. Deb knew how to work a courtroom and she knew how to work a crowd. She had them on their feet and in her hands, and she loved it and the crowd loved her right back. She kept it short and built to a huge, "So get out there! Get everyone you can to vote! Now, let's get something done!"

She dropped the mic and stepped back. The dancing judges formed a kick line and the crowd went crazy.

Deb was grinning as she came back to me, grabbed Slasher and comforted the pup, who was trembling from all the noise.

"Let's get out of here, BB," she said. "Leave 'em on their feet. Can't get any better than that."

We slipped out of the backstage area and headed toward an alley that led back toward *Hoosier Daddy*. Behind us, a sudden squeal ripped from the mic, followed by several bangs, as if the mic was being slammed against the stage. We turned around, looking back across the square toward the stage.

As the dancing judges had left, Harry Felcher and his rabble had swarmed onto the stage, holding signs proclaiming, "God Hates Fags", "Repent Before the Fire", and "Vengeful God". One even held a burning cross. Holy

KKKrazy, Batman! Felcher had wrestled the microphone from the MC and shouted, "Burn in the hellfire that God will rain down to cleanse the sinner! All sodomites and their fallen women will burn!"

I was too stunned to point out that hellfire, by most accounts, should come from below, so raining down should not be an option.

Deb started forward, back toward the square. I knew she would barrel onto that stage and confront Felcher. I reached to stop her, even though I had little hope of doing so. Waving a limp wrist at a buffalo stampede is a good definition of ineffectiveness. This was not going to end well.

Then Petunia stepped out of the shadows and blocked the path. She held out a hand like a traffic cop.

"Nope. Bad move."

Deb halted, but with plenty of f o r w a r d momentum stored. She rose on her toes, ready and very much willing to continue her plunge toward Felcher.

"Give me one good reason or get out of my way!"

Petunia was unmoved. Good description. Petunia was the essence of immovability. "I'll give you three. One, this shows what a whack job Felcher is. That shows everyone what your opposition looks like. They can see how important it is they get their butts out to vote. Two, the police are on the edge of the crowd and already moving in. They'll be busting everyone in a couple of minutes, and you don't want to get swept up in that."

Petunia didn't continue, so Deb asked, "And the third reason?"

The corner of Petunia's mouth twitched. I knew her enough to understand this was the Petunia version of a wide smile. "You'll upset Aunt May."

Deb looked at Petunia, then understood that something was afoot. She shrugged and nodded. We turned and continued back to her car, parked near *Hoosier Daddy*. No one saw us, except Petunia, who ambled along, about a half block back.

At her car, Deb stopped and squeezed my shoulder. "Except for Felcher, that was good, BB. Hang in there. Just another week. We have the fundraiser tomorrow night, Halloween on Friday, canvassing on the weekend, and the final rally on Monday with the Dems. It's almost done. You've done good. Take the day off tomorrow. Sleep in and meet me at the restaurant before Foxy's fundraiser. I've got a lot to thank that man for."

She got in the car and started it. I realized what was in my hand. "Deb," I said, knocking on the window. She rolled it down. I held out the briefcase. "Your purse." She winked and took it.

"Not a purse. It's a symbol. I can't exactly walk around with a gavel."

"You don't walk around with either. I do. A gavel would be lighter."

"You'll live. It will build up your upper body strength. Really, you should thank me."

I let that slide and just waved as she drove away. Then I turned toward home. My bed was calling me.

Chapter Twelve
The Break-in

At least they didn't wake me up this time. I wasn't even halfway through my primping for bed when the phone rang. I considered ignoring it. It was Roger. I considered some more. But I knew Roger. If he wanted me, he knew where the redial button was, and he wasn't afraid to use it. I sighed.

"Get down here."

"And it's nice to hear from you, too, Roger. How are you this splendid evening? Yes, I *was* just about to get into bed, so I'll just pop in and call you tomorrow."

"Shut up, BB. Get down here. Now."

There was a muted exchange and Deb came on. She sounded . . . deflated. I had never heard her so quiet, it chilled me. "BB, I'm sorry."

"Deb! What's wrong? Are you okay? What happened?"

"You better come down here. I'm . . . I'm sorry.

But I need you. We need to figure out—"

Roger came back on the line. "Is she hurt?" I yelled.

"Don't ask. Drive. Get here as fast as your limited repertoire of talents can manage. Pick up Nacho behind *Daddy's*."

"But what is going on?"

"Nacho's waiting. Get down here. You'll see."

He hung up. I stared at the phone. It wasn't telling me anything. I knew I could call back, but I also knew that Roger wasn't going to tell me any more. In addition, I knew Nacho was waiting, and Nacho was not one to be kept waiting. I sighed and got dressed. In a few minutes, I was pulling up behind *Daddy's*. Nacho was standing in the alley. "Do you know what's going on?"

Nacho lit a cigar, filling the car with gut-wrenching fumes. I rolled down the windows and proceeded to cough up a lung. "Drive," was the only response.

I drove.

We pulled up outside Deb's house. Again, all the flood lights were on. A small group was gathered around the barn that stood across the drive, opposite the house. We got out and approached. On the door of the barn, a small rag doll had been run through with a very large hunting knife. The knife had ripped through the doll's chest, pinning it to the weathered wooden door. Underneath, in red paint, someone had scrawled,

Your Next Bitch!
Give up or Die Tomorrow!

The red paint dripped like blood in a cheesy horror flick. Malevolent intent radiated from the tableau. Somehow the use of "your" instead of "you're" made it worse. This was someone skilled at mayhem and uncaring about the niceties of spelling. This was not a being who could be reasoned with or expected to behave with human decency. This was an act of base aggression.

Deb had her arms crossed over her chest. She seemed diminished.

"I've had that doll since I was little," she said quietly. "She was on a shelf in my bedroom. My bedroom upstairs."

I looked at the door, expecting to see it broken open, glass that had just been replaced, shattered. Nothing was out of place. I looked at Roger, who shook his head. "Door was locked. Alarm was on. Nothing was disturbed. It's like a ghost did it. I have the system set to record and to ping me if it's ever turned off or someone breaks in. It never pinged. It was on all the time, but somehow, someone got in. They got into her bedroom. They grabbed the doll and got out and did this. Didn't leave a trace."

Nacho took all this in. Nacho had some experience with very bad and very powerful enemies. "Show me."

Roger took Nacho inside. I stayed outside with Deb. She was shaken. She silently clutched Slasher to her chest. For once, it was the little dog who was providing a calming reassurance. Deb was wound so tight, I didn't want to touch her. I was afraid I would not sooth so much as make her crumble or lash out. She was not someone to be easily scooped into enveloping arms. *She* was the one who was supposed to be solid. I was supposed to be all atwitter, which I was. So, I stood and twitched, waiting for the grownups to decide what to do. Petunia paced around the yard, watching, ready to pounce if she spotted anything out of place.

Roger and Nacho came out. "Whoever did this knew what they were doing," Nacho said. "It ain't impossible, but it took skill. Nothin' like the crap head who attacked last night."

"Agreed," Roger said. "The only one of our suspects who has this kind of knowledge might be BurntHam. He's built some high-end estates, so should know his way around a security system."

"Not so fast," Deb said. "The preacher may have a follower who works in security. Then there's Judge Hawthorne. He's had burglars in his court. I should know ... I've defended a few."

"But they wouldn't come after you, would they?" I asked. "You helped them."

Deb shook her head. "A job is a job. If the judge offered enough money or a get-out-of-jail-free card next time they saw him, it's more than possible they'd take it."

"Don't care who it was," Nacho said. "The important thing is that you can't stay here. That's what the doll is for. If they just wanted to prove they could get in, they could have taken a dump on your kitchen floor. The message here is that they want you out of the race and they can get to you even where you feel safe. The way I see it, you've got two choices ... well, three. You can get police protection."

Deb shook her head. "Not happening. Wrong message and I don't want them snooping around."

Nacho nodded. "That's what I thought. Second option is to go somewhere where *we* can protect you."

"I don't like that idea. What is the third option?"

Nacho shrugged. "Drop out of the race like they said."

Deb growled. "I might consider that a few days after hell freezes over. No one is going to scare me out of this race." She considered. "I guess I'll have to go with Plan B. I have to admit that staying here isn't a good idea. I hate it, but I have my child to think of." She squeezed Slasher, who licked her face. Deb had gathered her wits and was climbing back into control. She looked at Roger and Nacho. "Do you have a place in mind?"

Roger spoke up, "We agree that Beau and Aunt May's house is best. They have the room. We won't have to surround it with watchers because—"

"I understand," Deb said.

Beau lived in what was generally known as the Ugly Thumb house because, well, it was old and ugly, and it stuck out like a sore thumb. Several years ago, when the city had planned a new police complex, with offices, a short-term jail, and several other cop- outrements, they had tried to acquire an entire block near campus through eminent domain. Most of the houses were student rentals and the owners were happy to get market value for houses that had been mishandled by scores of students and years of minimal maintenance. One house, however, still was home to Ms. Mavis Shakelford, the grand doyen of Magawatta culture, the daughter of a quarry owner, widow of a bank president, and professor emeritus of ballet in the prestigious Jeb Eden School of Music and Dance. The mayor and town council appointed a small committee to enter *the presence* and plead for permission to move the house to a new, classier location, of course at no cost to her. They were dispatched with shrieks of outrage, accompanied by tossed china and statuary. Madam Shakelford had been known as a severe mistress of the dance and age had not mellowed her.

The police complex was built around the house, with headquarters directly north and official parking and assorted garages behind. Throwing a bone to the neighborhood preservationists, the area to the south of the house was turned into a small park with a playground. A lawsuit by Mavis, because of the noise and traffic, led to the city picking up the tab for soundproofing the house. Once installed, the soundproofing increased the sense of separation between inside and out. While the outside was surrounded by a parking lot and police related buildings, crossing the threshold was like stepping into a perfect example of late nineteenth century plush. The outside of the house was ignored and allowed to slowly disintegrate, and the inside looked like it had been frozen in Lucite and installed in the Smithsonian. Beau answered an ad for a houseboy many years ago, when Ms. Mavis, as he called her, had decided she needed some personal help around the house. They soon discovered a mutual love for liquor and biting commentary. When she died, Ms. Shakelford left explicit instructions in her will that Beau was to have use of the house rent free for as long as he wished with the caveat that he had to maintain the "collection of artifacts" as she called the furnishings of the house. This included several priceless pieces of furniture and some irreplaceable items of dance history. The will specified that should anyone dare contest the will or should anyone ever attempt to evict Beau, the entire estate would immediately become his. As a result, Beau was regularly feted by the school in hopes that they might be the recipient of at least a part of the estate at some future moment of Beau's choosing.

The reason Nacho and Roger selected the Ugly Thumb house was because it stood alone, surrounded by police, cameras, and floodlights all day and night. There was no yard to speak of and no fence. Neither Ms. Shakelford nor Beau had any use for gardening. The only plants were the huge stands of bamboo along the street that threatened to make the front walk impenetrable. Planted years ago with a long - abandoned idea of creating a mediation garden screened from the constant flow of students, the bamboo was attempting to envelop the house. In time, it would succeed. The fence on the sides and back had fallen into disrepair decades ago and were removed during the construction of what the students called 'the pig pen'. The front door, while ornate, was oak covering a steel core. Even the mail slot beside the door opened only into a small, safe - like steel box. This had been installed after a drunken fraternity prank involving a snake. Every time in all the years that Beau or I had stumbled the two blocks between our houses when we had reached our personal tipping point, we always saw at least one police car. We were known to them and categorized as innocuous. We weren't bothered, but we were noticed.

No one was going to get to Deb if she was staying in the Ugly Thumb.

Roger called Beau and after several attempts, managed to rouse him from his stupor and inform him of the plan. It would have been easier to wake Aunt May, but she eschewed cell phones. "I do not want anyone and everyone to be able to reach out and touch me at any time in any place," she said when asked. "I do not mind being touched in a variety of places and locales, but I wish to be able to decide on the place and placement. One must maintain a certain distance and decorum, I believe. Otherwise, there is no allure."

Beau knew better than to protest when Nacho or Roger commanded and shortly we were in the parlor. "Nacho and I will focus on tracking our main suspects," Roger said. "Aunt May, have you made any inroads with the preacher?"

Aunt May nodded but did not say any more. We knew from past experience that the difficulty of stopping Aunt May when she was loquacious was matched only by the futility of trying to pry information from her before she chose to speak. Roger looked at her, debating whether an attempt to encourage her to expound would reap more details or not. After a moment he gave up, sighed, and turned to Deb. I was amazed and amused. Roger allowed few people to dictate to him or even hint he go in a particular direction. Nacho was granted the right grudgingly. Petunia's suggestions were considered. My opinion was met with bemused indifference. However, it seemed Aunt May was one of the rarefied elite in Roger's world.

Roger turned back to Deb. "My dear, I know you don't want to, but you need to stay put tomorrow. Stay here. Don't go out. I want to throw everything we have on digging out the person behind this. If we can get them, we can make them call off their killers.

Please tell me you are not going to give me any grief about this. We can't follow you and root out this asshole, too. We don't have enough people."

Deb was still shaken. She sat stroking Slasher. "I hate it, but there is brave and there is stupid. I'll stay here tomorrow. But tomorrow night ..."

"You absolutely must go to Foxy's fundraiser," I said. "If you don't appear there, you might as well drop out.

Deb nodded. "I agree. I can't miss it."

"Foxy rented *Fields and Streams*, that new fru-fru restaurant," Roger said. "It's not a large place and there won't be a stage. Deb will be meeting people one on one and the guests are all known to Foxy, so it should be relatively safe." He turned to Nacho. "Are your friends in town yet?"

"First batch arrived a little while ago. I've already talked with Foxy. We'll have a dozen scattered through the place."

I looked at Deb, expecting an explosion for their interference. She certainly would have blown her top yesterday. What a difference a knife makes She said nothing, just continued to stroke Slasher. She was truly and deeply shaken.

Nacho sighed and stood. "It's been a long night. Deb, you should try to get some sleep. We'll go back to the *Café* and flesh out details for tomorrow."

"Shouldn't someone stay and watch the house?"

Beau asked.

Roger shook his head. "We need to focus our attention on finding the perpetrator. We don't have unlimited resources or unlimited time. You should be safe. You have more police within shouting distance than anywhere else in town. I doubt anyone is either that good or stupid enough to try anything here."

Aunt May stood and went to Deb. "You come upstairs, dear. You're in the blue room. It's got a lovely bed, but not too high, so your protector can jump down if he needs to investigate anything." She gently scratched Slasher, then led Deb out of the room.

"Go on home, BB," Roger said. "Your ability to plan is questionable and you get a bit too bitchy when you don't get enough beauty rest. We'll call if we need you. Get to the soiree early tomorrow night. Until then, fly . . . be free."

I didn't wait for anyone to change their mind. I blew a kiss in Beau's direction and was out the door.

Chapter Thirteen
Wednesday Night

I got to the restaurant with plenty of time to help before the doors opened. However, the Felcherites got there before me. They filled the sidewalk, carrying torches and crosses. All they needed were some white robes and it would have looked like a good ol' time Klan rally. Of course, the 'God Hates Fags' and 'You Shall be Judged' signs were not traditional, but the hate behind them was. Felcher was in fine form, with a megaphone in one hand and the Bible in the other. "This trollop of Satan will burn. Fire shall consume her and all those who flock to her. Shun her for the flames of Hell are real!" His face bulged in the torchlight. He looked like he might burst into flame just to prove his point. I waded through them. At the door to the restaurant I looked back at the crowd, trying to somehow pick out any potential assassins. No one had a neon sign above them that read '*Caution: Killer Below*'. Then I blinked, stunned. Very close to Felcher, untroubled and untouched by the waves of hate, a hand resting gently on his butt, was Aunt May. She gave no indication that she knew me, merely serenely gazed back. I'm not the sharpest pencil in the box, but it occurred to me that I had better stop looking her way or someone was going to notice and that was not going to help her ingratiate herself into the horde. I shook off my shock and stumbled into the restaurant. Deb was gazing out the door while a mixture of disgust, amusement, and anger battled across her face.

"What are we going to do about the uninvited?" I asked.

"Not much to do," Deb saidd. "They'd love to have

someone call the cops. They'll yell freedom of speech and the news will cover them, not me. They still will probably get most of the press. Loud imbeciles are more interesting than a lesbian judge."

"I can think of a few ladies who would prefer you," I said with a hint of a leer.

"I said more interesting, not preferable," Deb said and winked. "Let's go help Foxy get ready. Maybe we can get some of the event staff to help arrivals run the gauntlet."

However, just beyond the entryway, it became clear that Foxy had everything well under control. This evening was Foxy's show and he was not about to be upstaged. This man had opened *Pie Holes* across the country and knew how to prepare for nearly any eventuality. "If a small demonstration by backwoods born-agains can stymie this event, I might as well go back to the bayou," he said to us. "I have prepared for this and several other eventualities." He returned to speaking into his phone, while his assistant, Rox was busy on another. As we watched, a large truck pulled up outside loaded with rolls of plastic tarp-like material over twelve feet tall. Another truck contained a load of fourteen-foot-tall, shiny metal poles. A short bus pulled up and out of it streamed two very different groups. The first were construction guys. They went to work immediately, setting up the poles. The base of each pole was bolted to large metal plates which were pulled out of the trucks and laid on the street and sidewalk. Those poles weren't going anywhere. Each one took three men with très butch wrenches to erect and would take more than that to bring down. At the top of each pole, a strong, directed floodlight flashed on, brightly lighting the area in front of the pole while leaving the area behind the pole in darkness. Trailing down from each bright light were several flashing colored lights.

Very festive!

Next, the workmen unrolled the plastic tarp material and it was splendid to see. Printed on the tarps were huge, billboard-sized banners with pictures of Deb in many poses, from looking judicial to kissing a baby. Winding through the enormous pictures were slogans and quotes and, oft repeated, the specific judicial position she was seeking, the date of the election, and a myriad of exhortations to vote and make sure everybody they knew voted, no matter what horrendous obstacles stood in their way.

As this was going up, the second wave of people came off the bus. Drag queens, drag kings, transitioners aplenty, and a big ol' bunch of supporters of all ilks. They looked fabulous. Each was outfitted with a portable loudspeaker plus flyers, buttons, and candy, oh my. Each pole had two or more supporters standing by, greeting guests and waving them inside.

The words and fervor of the Felcherites were hidden behind the barrier. It was wonderful, but Foxy had a bit of frosting to add. He had installed a few clear plastic "windows" in the barriers. The Felcherites clustered there, shouting and holding up their signs. However, what they didn't see were the placards Foxy had emblazoned above and below the windows which proudly proclaimed, 'Indiana Idioticus! Feeds on Hate! Caution: Dangerous. Inbreeding Program Currently Underway'.

Within twenty minutes, the new entryway was constructed and the guests began to arrive, shuttled from off site parking and escorted to the door, while marveling at the wondrous show. Foxy, completely relaxed, smiled broadly and introduced each arriving guest to Deb. Soon the restaurant was full. From past experience, invitees knew that Foxy's soirees started on time and being late was a sure way to not be invited to the next event. There was no formal seating, but places aplenty to sit, lean or perch. Hunky waiters continuously circulated with trays laden with drinks, nibbles and wonderful food.

I didn't have much to do. Deb mingled and chatted with the donors. She actually enjoyed doing that. For me, coming up with something to say to near strangers in social situations lurched between tedious and excruciating. So, I did what I usually do when I can't avoid attendance. I found a quiet place to observe, at the ready should my particular talents be wanted or needed. Luckily, there was little danger of that. The Glasstown quartet was playing their quiet, intricate songs as background music. The attendees were far above my place in the social order, so I didn't know anyone except by reputation and they had no interest in knowing me. I was happy to sit quietly, sharing my plate of expensive and artsy food with Slasher while I gazed appreciatively at the waiters passing through the crowd. The briefcase sat at my feet, should Deb ask for it. I was attempting to rank the waiters in order of personal preference. As I had time, I was subdividing them into various contests, from poise and presentation while bending over to pick up a dropped napkin, to overall appearance in and out of uniform, to needing my help to deal with a persistent erection that was ruining the perfect lines of their uniform. Competition was fierce and kept a smile playing across my lips, although my eyes had glazed over a bit. Outside of the sewer that was my mind, the party was impressive. Foxy had reached out to everyone in town he had ever done a favor for, and Foxy's favors were many and generous. The elite of Magawatta art, education, research, business, finance, and more hobnobbed with each other and Deb.

"It is not the money raised that is important,"

Foxy explained to Deb when he proposed putting on the party and, of course, footing the bill. "The event will likely cost more than it brings in because I insist that the food and drink be excellent. Rubber chickens have their place, but that place is alongside seltzer bottles in clown shows, not on plates at fundraisers. The reason for requiring donations is that every person who contributes will become an ardent supporter."

"But won't they feel their money entitles them to special consideration?" Deb asked.

"If they give too much, certainly," Foxy answered. "The trick is to ask for the correct amount. Too little is like giving change to a panhandler. One does it to make someone go away or assuage a feeling of guilt. Too much and the giver feels they have purchased something.

However, a significant, but not extravagant donation makes the giver a fervent promoter. They want to feel their money made a difference and that they made a good choice. They want to be sure they didn't back the wrong horse. Of course, I am not comparing you to a horse, my dear. They want bragging rights, not special treatment. Only the most coarse and miserly think a few hundred dollars will buy that. So, a personal thank you and a nod to them for being on your team is all that is necessary. They will be certain to get out and vote, as well as get all their friends to do the same."

Foxy knew more about the allure and power that money did and more importantly, did not possess than anyone else we knew. We all took his advice when talk turned to such things and had never been disappointed.

Nacho grunted into a chair beside me. I rarely saw Nacho outside of the P*atio Café* and certainly could not recall seeing the muumuu bedecked owner in another restaurant. However, as each of the waiters passed, they nodded in our direction and quickly found the time to stop by and whisper a few words in Nacho's ear. I realized these were the "foot" soldiers of the Twinkie Army that Nacho had summoned. The waiters were not pretty faces trying to hustle up some easy cash—a demographic which had provided me not a few joyful evenings. That realization reduced the pleasure of ranking the boys. They were already working more than one job and surveillance took precedence. Dalliance was not even on the menu. So, while upon other occasions I have taken home a tired, cute waiter who enjoyed my repartee, I knew these were beholden to a higher calling. Nevertheless, the boys *were* extraordinarily good looking and in tip-top shape, and even if I cannot take home a painting, I can still enjoy looking at it.

Relieved of the effort of maintaining a glamorous and interesting exterior, I turned to Nacho to get the latest news. "I haven't heard anything from Roger. How goes the search for the bad guy?"

Nacho stared at me long enough to make me uncomfortable. "BB, are you actually trying to make small talk with me or is there something you need to know? I'm doing something here and I'm sitting because my leg hurts."

Of course I had been making small talk, but didn't want to admit to wasting Nacho's time. "Well, I thought maybe I should be looking out for—"

Nacho interrupted me. "How about this. Watch out for anyone coming at you with a gun, knife, or large object and tell me if that happens. Wait, let me correct that. Watch for anyone coming at Deb. If they're coming at you, you can do whatever you want."

"I'm sorry, Nacho. I'm not used to all this . . . this . . . ." I didn't really know what to call it. This was not excitement. This was danger. This was living outside my comfortably dull and predictable existence.

Nacho relented. "You'll be okay, BB. We're on it. Roger has heard about some very interesting meetings that BurntHam, our developer friend, has had with a group of landowners at the lake. Evidently, he's roped in a boatload of cash, but still has to come up with a pile more than he has. He's borrowed against everything he has any claim to and is juggling too many moving pieces. If it falls apart, he's ruined. In my experience, people in that position are willing to do anything to keep their ass safe and he's one dickhead who didn't have a lot of scruples to begin with. We're trying to run down which of his employees have the skills to break through a security system. So, he's still very much on the list. Roger has also been checking into the employees of the company that runs Deb's security system."

"I thought Roger ran her security."

"Roger designed it and did some upgrades. He keeps a second eye on the place, but he doesn't want to monitor her place all the time. He had her contract out regular monitoring. That's grunt work and he's not in love with that kind of assignment. None of you are."

"We tend to follow our interests."

"You tend to wander aimlessly in search of boys and booze, but that's beside the point. We checked out the security company when she first signed up, but Roger is trying to find out if someone has been exercising some quiet leverage over any of the workers. If any of them has had any legal problems, the judge is in a good position to take advantage of that."

"You really think Hawthorne is behind this?"

"I don't know and until we have more information, it would be stupid to focus on one person. I don't do stupid. I do know that the judge has been reaching out to his fellow Republicans. He's doing it quietly. He ain't asking for anything special. Just wants to keep the door open in case something happens to Deb."

"That sounds like he has an idea that something is up. How could he know that unless he was the one causing it?"

Nacho rapped me on the head. "Think, BB. He's been a judge for a long time. The cops in town like him. If you think he doesn't have friends who let him know what's going on as soon as it happens, then you're dumber than I give you credit for."

I sighed. "And I suppose that our torch-bearer out front is still on the list."

Nacho grunted. "Three of his flock are security installers. The job at Deb's needed more brains than the numbnut who tried to shoot her, but there don't seem to be a shortage of people with the skills to do it. So, no. No one is off our list."

From the crowd of people clustering around Deb, raised voices attracted my attention.

"I *said* I will not comment on a potential case. I can't make a decision until I've heard the arguments. That is what a judge does. She judges." Deb was obviously not happy.

"Listen, you bitch. I paid good money to come here and I do not spend money for nothing. I expect an answer and it better be the right one."

"I just gave you my answer, Mr. Burns. And if you think donating to my campaign buys you something more than my thanks, you do not understand me, the political process, or the law."

"Nobody crosses me and gets away with it. You

better watch yourself, dyke. Stand in my way and I'll take you down. I don't fight to just win. I'll rip your damn throat out."

The whole place had become suddenly very quiet. Quiet crowds are frightening. It's that moment when you are pretty sure something really unpleasant is about to happen, and you don't want to miss a single awful thing.

I hurried over, pushing my way through the crowd. Most people in town knew what BurntHam – I mean Hamilton Burns – looked like. With his silver hair, expensive black suit, and manicured nails, he could have made a good living renting himself out as a stand-in for corporate CEO publicity photos. Yet, despite all the fluffing that money could buy, nothing could be done to hide the greedy eyes and cheap dive brawler twist to his mouth. If you dropped a dollar, he'd take it. Not because he needed it, but because he could and if you called him on it, he'd deny it. If he got caught, he'd fight rather than admit he was wrong. He was standing very close to Deb, obviously trying to intimidate her. This indicated he didn't know her or didn't care and was too stupid to recognize someone who could not be intimidated by the likes of him.

Deb had settled into her street fighting pose. I had seen her do this only a couple of times—once at *Daddy's* when some frats had invaded and wanted to beat up some fags to prove how straight and manly they were, and once in court when a prosecutor had attempted to rip apart her client, a woman who had been charged with battery when she had attacked her abusive husband. Deb had taken apart the prosecutor with her objections, using words and logic, until the man was in tears and the judge had to call a recess. The frats were not clever enough to understand her logic, so she had knocked all three of them silly and was in the process of eviscerating them when Nacho stepped in and saved their lives.

I was in a quandary. Stepping in between them would be more dangerous than stepping between a matador and a charging bull. I had no love for BurntHam, but I didn't think Deb's campaign would be helped by a charge of manslaughter or, in this particular case, ass slaughter. I was saved from having to make a decision when Foxy injected himself into the situation. Foxy was elegant. Foxy was gay. Foxy also towered above both of them. He put a collegial arm around Burns's shoulders.

"Ah, Hamilton, my dear. I am most sorry. I believe I must have misrepresented what this evening was all about. Let's get you your money back and scoot you on home so you won't have to call the evening a complete waste. However, I do insist you take home a bottle of this most divine Oliver Pinot Noir as my apology for inconveniencing you. It is the 2014 and they only produced 300 cases." He was moving Burns toward the door as he spoke. He raised a hand to one of the waiters, who quickly handed him a bottle. Foxy pressed the bottle into Burns's hands, forcing him to unclench his fists. Foxy pulled a large roll of bills from his pocket and peeled off two, crisp, one-hundred-dollar bills, which he tucked into Burns's shirt pocket. They were at the door. "Wonderful to see you again, Hamilton. Look, here's your car. I had the boy bring it around from parking. Again, please accept my deepest apologies." And with that, Foxy guided BurntHam out the door, to his car, held the door for him, closed it firmly, and stood in the street until Burns drove off. Foxy returned to the restaurant, which was still holding its collective breath. He spoke over the silence, "Don't you just hate it when you are expecting champagne and are served wine coolers?" He turned to his beloved Suave. "Would you favor us with a song, my love? Perhaps *Goody Goody*. That always makes me smile and seems somehow apropos."

Suave nodded and slipped to the microphone.

Soon, Malneck and Mercer's catty, funny song wiped the unpleasantness from the air. After Suave's elegant voice faded from the final note and the crowd applauded her performance, Glasstown launched into another song and conversation resumed. Deb began to work the crowd again. I breathed a sigh of relief and went back to my chair, which Slasher had been keeping warm.

The rest of the evening passed without any excitement or really any need for me. I drank a few free drinks, ate a bit of free food, and napped. No one was interested in talking to me. I was obviously below their place on the food chain. I do not mind being ignored in these situations. I do not feel any need to be seen and appreciated. I was content to let the evening pass without the excitement that had been buffeting me over the last few days.

Round about midnight the last of the guests trickled out. I thanked Foxy and bid Deb adieu.

"I'm still staying at Beau and May's," said Deb. "Take tomorrow off. Go to your real job for a change. I'll see you on Friday at *Daddy's* for Halloween. TiaRa is putting me on about ten. The place should be packed by then, but it will be early enough that folks won't be too drunk to understand what I'm saying. It won't take long, but it's important. Will you be wearing a costume?"

"No. No way I can match what the true devotees will be wearing, so I'll be an appreciative audience. See you then." I handed over Slasher and her briefcase and headed home.

Chapter Fourteen
The Fire

At two-thirty in the morning, I was wrenched out of a lovely fantasy by my phone ringing. It was Beau.

Strange. He was usually passed out or nearly so by this time and thankfully he was not inclined to initiate drunken heart to heart conversations. I punched accept and suddenly he was screaming in my ear.

"It's burning! BB! Everything's on fire. I can't. I don't. BB, get here. The flames. The smoke!"

Beau tends to the hysterical easily. I could tell there was a fire, but it could be a piece of toast. I tried to channel calm. "Beau, what's on fire? Do you know where the fire extinguisher is?"

"The house. The whole house is on fire! Help!"

At this point, I heard sirens outside. I looked out my front window and saw a fire engine tear down the street toward Beau's. Maybe he wasn't exaggerating. "Beau, are you in the house? Are you trapped? Is everybody out?"

Beau was hyperventilating. "I'm out. Deb woke me and we both got out. The downstairs is all burning. It's all burning, BB."

"What about May?"

"Still upstairs. I banged on her door but it was locked, and Deb was pulling me out and I have to go back in and get her but—"

At this point Deb grabbed the phone. I heard her use her most commanding voice. "Beau! Sit down. You are about to pass out. Sit. Now!" She spoke into the phone. "BB, the firemen are here. Aunt May will be all right. She must have had a little too much to drink. We couldn't wake her, but there's a fire escape to her window and the firemen are going up there as we speak. The fire hasn't reached up there."

"What about you? You can't be out on the street. Someone could take a shot at you like that meth head did."

"There are police all over. It's in their friggin' backyard. Firemen, too. It's a bit of a zoo. I'll be okay. Roger's on his way and he's calling Nacho. You should get over here."

"On my way," I said and disconnected. I grabbed clothes, paying no attention to looking fabulous. What does the discerning homo wear to a fire, anyway? There is a time and place for fashion, and this was not one of them. I grabbed my coat and actually ran the two blocks to Beau's house. By the time I arrived, the hoses were uncoiled and three gushers of water were blasting the flames. It was already obvious that the water was winning. The windows of the downstairs had shattered and there was scorching, but the flames were quickly dying.

I ran to Beau and he threw himself into my arms, weeping. I was freaked, but Beau was so hysterical that I felt the picture of calm, cool, and collected next to his quivering meltdown. I held him, patting his back and saying the inane things about everything being okay that everybody does in these situations— even when it is absolutely impossible to know what, if anything was going to be okay. However, I figure that such lies are more soothing than either truthful assessment or telling your loved one to shut the fuck up. So, I patted him and said that it would be okay. His sobs continued, but he let go of me and sank down onto the grass, arms covering his head, rocking back and forth, moaning and sobbing. I knew Beau well enough to know he was basically all right. Once he gathered his wits about him, he would find a bottle of something and drink himself into a nice, quiet coma and wake up tomorrow with enough ironic distance to figure out how to proceed. All he needed was some time. All he needed from me was liquor, a place to consume it, and a bed to lie in after he had reached either his limit or the bottom of the bottle . ... and he rarely reached a limit.

I looked over at Deb. She was obviously in shock and running on automatic. Thankfully, Deb's automatic was a very stolid, functional thing, contrasting nicely with Beau. She stood watching the firemen work, stroking Slasher, who was quivering in her arms. Two policemen were talking with her and she was answering with mostly one- or two-word replies. I heard a lot of "I have no idea," and "No. Nothing." They finally gave up and started interviewing people who had gathered to watch.

Deb looked at me, then gestured with her chin back at the house. I saw a small group coming down the rickety, metal fire escape that clung to the side of the house, reaching to the second floor. I saw a fireman in full regalia at the front and two more in the rear. As they stepped off the ladder and separated, I saw Aunt May walking between them wrapped in a blanket. It had slipped down exposing a bare shoulder. Then I noticed another blanket-wrapped person moving behind her as if she could be a shield from prying eyes. The person was looking around like a cornered animal, crouching and bobbing. Then the group stepped into the flood-lit area at the front of the house and he was revealed.

It was the Reverend Felcher. Obviously, Aunt May had succeeded in injecting herself into the Reverend's followers, or vice versa. As Mrs. Reverend Felcher was not a party to the party, I quickly understood the reason for his furtive demeanor. At this moment, a local television news van pulled up and a reporter and cameraman piled out. Even in the glaring light of floods, I could see Felcher's face pale and he let out a scream, pulled the blanket over his head, and took off running. A brief gust of wind billowed the blanket, giving me an unwelcome glimpse of very white, spindly legs and a naked, saggy butt before he plunged through some bushes that separated the Ugly Thumb from the park and was gone. Aunt May watched him go, then turned to her rescuers, who I could tell even from this distance were fine specimens of firemen, emphasis on the *men*. She looked them up and down, then I saw her hand fly to her forehead. She pulled an exaggerated faint, allowing the hunkiest one to catch her. I smiled and turned away. Aunt May was obviously fine and whatever Felcher had done had not sated her desires, merely inflamed them—which, given the situation, seemed appropriate.

I turned and saw Roger and Petunia hurrying up. Nacho was farther away, clumping along, leaning on the ever-present walking stick and puffing a foul cigar. Roger went to us. Petunia continued toward the house, shrugging off two firemen and three policemen who were stopping anyone from getting close.

"What happened?" Roger asked. "Anybody hurt?"

"Everyone is fine," Deb answered. "Well, Beau is having a major melodramatic meltdown, but we can't fault him for that. Slasher needed to go out, so I got up and saw"

It seemed like the enormity of someone finding her and being willing to set fire to Beau's house within spitting distance of the entire Magawatta police force hit her all at once. Deb froze. Then something in her face crumbled and she started shaking, rocking back and forth, whispering to Slasher.

Roger stepped forward and scooped her into a strong hug. Then, he kept an arm around her and started walking her back toward his car. Nacho was just coming up to us. One look at Deb and Roger and it was clear what was going on. "Get her to the safe house. You know the one," Nacho said.

Roger nodded and continued toward the cars. Nacho glared at me. Of course, that was Nacho's general look of greeting. "I'll tell you where it is later, BB, but if you ever speak the address aloud to anyone or communicate it in any way, I will personally pull your tongue out of your mouth and hand it to you. Do you understand?"

I nodded.

"Good. Now, where is Petunia? She'll be able to figure out what had happened."

I looked toward the house and saw the glacial glide of Petunia head in our direction. Walking up, she ignored me and addressed Nacho. "They couldn't break in. Would have made too much noise. Couldn't do anything around the back. They poured gas in through the mail slot, then tossed in a match. Some damage and lots of smoke. Would have been extremely lucky to do anything more. My guess, it was done to scare and send a message that they can hit wherever they want."

Nacho nodded. "We should have had someone watching the house."

Petunia shrugged. "Limited resources. Better to focus on finding the head of the snake. That's what we were doing."

"Fire makes me think of the Reverend," Nacho said. "He loves to spout shit about hellfire raining down on the unbeliever. He'd call this the hand of God. More likely the hand of one of Felcher's storm troopers."

"No. It wasn't Felcher," I said. "No way."

They both looked at me.

"What do you mean?" Nacho asked. "How can you be so sure? You're not sure about what color shirt to wear most days."

"You didn't see him sneak away?" I asked. They looked at me blankly. What a satisfying feeling. I knew something that neither Petunia nor Nacho did. I would have loved to lord it over them, to stretch out the story like I would during the retelling I could already imagine during a Sunday afternoon confab at *Nacho Mama's Patio Café* when the friends gathered to drink and dish about the previous week. However, one look at Nacho and Petunia made it clear that beating around the bush would lead to a beating for me, not the bush, so I quickly described Felcher's appearance and rapid disappearance. We looked over toward Aunt May, who was leaning heavily on her chosen fireman, one hand seemingly randomly massaging his privates.

"We'll confirm with May later," Nacho said. "She

looks busy now, but you're right. Even his followers aren't so stupid that they would set fire to the house he was in."

"Maybe they didn't know." Petunia suggested. "No," Nacho stated. "He knows how dumb they are. He'd make sure they cleared it with him before they did anything that could get him in trouble."

Petunia nodded. "Makes sense."

Nacho looked at me. "BB, take Beau to your house for tonight. Petunia, you mind hanging here to see if anything else shakes out?"

Petunia shook her head. "Fine by me. I'll watch after Aunt May, too. From what I saw, her room wasn't damaged, so they'll probably let her back in." She glanced over at Aunt May, who was now laying on the ground with her head in the fireman's lap. "Of course, from what I see, she may be going back to the firehouse."

Nacho grunted. "That boy better watch out. That old lady will snap his spine. I've got to check on a few things. Then I'll go talk to Roger and Deb. We'll keep her on ice for now. Once I get back to the *Café*, I'll send one of my people to relieve you and watch the house." Petunia nodded.

Nacho turned and headed off, then called back, "BB, get Beau out of here. I don't want him whining to the police. They'll insist on talking to Deb and I want to keep her safe. We'll all get together at the *Café* tomorrow afternoon at five. I'll call you if the time changes."

"Should I call you if anything comes up?"

Nacho turned and stared at me. It made me uncomfortable. "You don't have my number, do you?"

"Umm . . . no, but you could give it to me."

"You don't need my number. You can call Roger. You can call the *Café*. You *cannot* call me. Understood?"

I gulped and nodded. Nacho turned and clumped away.

It was late. I was freaked. I went to Beau and helped him up. I decided this would be a good night to join him for a cocktail or ten.

Chapter Fifteen
Your Presence is Requested

I finally had a few minutes to myself. Deb was securely ensconced in one of Nacho's safe houses. I didn't know where it was, nor did I want to. Beau woke up far too cheerful for someone who had imbibed the amounts we both had sucked down. However, I knew from past experience that he was inexcusably untroubled by hangovers. I was not so blessed. He wasn't even upset about the damage to his house.

"It's insured, BB. Contents and structure. I believe this means I will be able to redo the entire downstairs, which means extended adventures in shopping on someone else's dime. What's not to love?" He went off to assess the damage and begin the process of rebuilding—something that I would have looked forward to as much as a dental extraction, but he joyously embraced.

Instead, I was treated to a very long phone call with Dustyn, my boss. He went on at great and painful length about what a hardship my, as he called them, *extracurricular activities* had caused him. "This is not a 'come in whenever you feel like it' office, BB," he scolded. "Our work is essential to the library. Crucial to its reputation. If you cannot rise to the level of professionalism required, perhaps it is time for you to look for other employment."

While I knew he would be hard-pressed to find someone with my education and experience for the salary he offered, the income was grand for me. More than that, I dreaded the prospect of looking for work even more than the continued annoyance of working for Dustyn.

"This is almost over," I said. "The election is on Tuesday. I'm sorry it is taking so much time, Dustyn. It wasn't in the plan to have fires and threats."

"Well, you should have planned better," he snipped.

I stifled the urge to unload the past days' frustrations upon his self-involved head. "I am truly sorry," I said, glad I was on the phone and only had to sound sincere, not look like I meant it. "I'll make sure everything you want is just right for the opening. We have enough time. I'll put in whatever hours it takes. Just let me get through this election. Then I'm all yours."

He sniffed again. "You know I can't afford to pay you overtime. I shouldn't have to, because *you* have caused this problem by spending all your time with *that woman*."

If I bit my tongue any harder, I was afraid I might draw blood. "I'll do it on my own time. There's absolutely no reason for you or your budget to suffer because of this. And Deb's campaign will help the community."

"Perhaps. I don't bother with politics myself, and steer clear of anything to do with courts. I have no interest in a bunch of miscreants and rowdies."

I shook my head but held my tongue.

"I promise I'll be there for part of the day tomorrow, even though it's Halloween. This weekend I'll work on the campaign. Monday is the last day of campaigning, but I'll come in for a couple of hours. Tuesday is the election and after that, all this will be over, and I promise I'll dedicate my entire life to getting the exhibition perfect."

He gave the sigh of a long-suffering Jewish mother about to tell her child not to worry about her, that she'd be all right. "I'm just a pushover," he moaned. "That's what I am. A pushover. I try to be strict, but I just can't do it. Go ahead. Have your fun.

I'll try to keep everything going by myself somehow." "Thank you, Dustyn. You are a special kind of person," I said, hopefully hiding the irony I felt. I was certain he would interpret my statement in the most complementary way.

I hung up and fell back into the overstuffed cushions. I had nothing required of me until our five o'clock meeting at Nacho's. My cat, Spot, took this as an invitation and leapt onto my lap, digging his claws into my leg in pre-appreciation of the strokes that better be on the way. I complied and allowed some of the bunched muscles in my shoulders to begin to relax. My eyes lowered and, with the loud rumbling from Spot soothing me, the scenes of fire and fright started to drift away.

BAM. BAM. BAM.

Someone at the door. Oh joy. Someone coming over without calling first. The way my life had been going, the chance that this was a delightful surprise instead of a new catastrophe was as likely as a visit from the Tooth Fairy, Santa, or a young stud.

BAM. BAM. BAM. Ah, unexpected, unwelcome, *and* impatient. "Madison County Sheriff's department. Open up." The voice was loud and officious. I wondered if that was something they taught at the academy or if it was something they screen for during pre-employment.

I got up. They weren't going away. Spot jumped off my lap and huffed off. I had failed as a human and there would be punishment in my future.

I opened the door. A uniformed man with a rather large gun on his hip looked me up and down and not in a 'mmm, who's this hunka hunka man?' sort of way. It was more a 'give me an excuse to slap the cuffs on this obvious deadbeat' look.

"Mr. Singer?"

How do they manage to make a completely innocent question sound like an accusation? I nodded, feeling guilty.

"I'm Officer Jenkins. The judge wants to have a word with you."

"Judge?" He nodded.

"What judge? Am I being arrested?"

"No. I am requesting that you accompany me of your own free will. Of course, if you refuse " He let the rest of the sentence dangle in the air, but I had a feeling neither he nor I would like it if I asked him to finish it.

"Let me call my lawyer."

He held up a hand. "Please. I have been instructed to request that you keep this meeting confidential. The judge will explain when you get there. I am to emphasize that you are not being arrested. This has nothing to do with a criminal proceeding."

I wasn't thrilled, but I was curious. I looked past him. On the street was a sheriff's car. He seemed legitimate. I figured with all the crazy things that had happened, this might just be some official follow-up. Besides, Magawatta is a small town. It's not a place where police or sheriffs made people disappear. At least, I hadn't heard of that happening. Of course, if they had disappeared, would anyone have heard of it? Oh well, if this was my time, it was my time. I shrugged. "Let me get my coat. I've got to be back for a meeting with Deb at five." This wasn't quite true, but I figured that it would be best to say I was going to be missed if I wasn't back soon.

Officer Jenkins nodded. "That will be no problem, sir. I'll bring you back in plenty of time."

So, off I went with the nice man in uniform. I even got to sit in the front seat of the cop car. There were handles on the inside of the door. I checked.

That was reassuring. I didn't know what was going on, but I was pretty sure I wasn't being taken out to be killed. We headed to the east side of town. It was an area of small developments, each one featuring a brick gateway emblazoned with a bucolic name and a water feature. Several had sprouted over the years. I never knew anyone who lived in one or aspired to do so. It was a part of Magawatta completely foreign to me. I only knew these things existed because I occasionally got lost in one by taking a wrong turn while trying to find the mall on one of my rare trips to the land of plastic retail. We pulled into the driveway of a tasteless McMansion barely distinguishable from the rest.

"This isn't Judge Walker's house," I said. The officer didn't reply. He just nodded toward the car door. "Whose house is this?" Again, there was no response.

Again, the officer nodded toward the car door. I sighed, opened the door, and climbed out. Then I noticed the officer was staying in the car. "Aren't you coming?"

"No sir. I will wait here. The meeting is to be private. I will be here to drive you home when you are finished."

"Who am I meeting?"

He gave a short shake of his head. "Just ring the bell. You are expected."

I sighed again. The events of the last few days had worn me down. I looked around. This was not exactly the set for a murder mystery. Suburbia may be horrifying, but only because of the décor. I had come this far. I wasn't going to try to make a run for it. I'm not big on running and he had a car. No benefit in making a fuss. The sooner this was over, the sooner I could get back to the couch.

I walked to the door and rang the bell. Ersatz Big Ben chimes sounded from inside. Such class. The door opened and there stood Judge Hawthorne, boy boffer and our "worthy" opponent. I had never had the displeasure of meeting him in person, although I had seen him looking judicial in publicity shots and looking embarrassed in newspaper shots after his arrest. Close up, his nose bloomed with the broken veins of a heavy drinker. One might call him bloated. To my eye, he looked overly inflated. While his face was soft and puffy, his eyes looked hard and spoke of unpleasant thoughts lurking within. Some would describe them as piggy. I, however, have never stared a real pig in the face. The judge's eyes had the fast calculation of a hooker. I bet he could guess my weight, income, and sexual preferences with a glance and be right on all three. *Paco Rabanne Eau de Parfum*, a popular but cheap scent billowed toward me, making my eyes tear. He was old, saggy, and just the right choice if someone had sent down to central casting for a corrupt old judge. He smiled and I stifled a gasp. It was not a nice smile. Thankfully, he did not hold out a hand to shake. I really didn't want to touch him. I briefly wondered what he had offered to those boys—it had to be significant.

"Mr. Singer, thank you for coming. Please come

in." The voice had once been a tenor but had devolved to somewhere between reedy and creaky. If the slowly closing door from every horror movie had been able to speak, it would have sounded like Judge Hawthorne.

I hesitated. I really did not want to be there and certainly didn't want to be alone with the man. However, I had to admit to being curious. What could he possibly want with me? I followed him inside.

The house was furnished in upper-middle-class tasteless. Large, overstuffed furniture, copious electronics, and lots of testaments to the judge's position and many accomplishments—pictures, awards and plaques, oh my.

He led the way into a living room and offered me a drink. For once I declined, thinking about roofies and several of the things I did not want to do with this guy. He directed me to a chair, then sat and poured himself a drink.

"I suppose you are wondering why you are here," he said.

I nodded.

"We may be able to help each other," he said.

"What do you mean?"

"I have been a judge for many years. We both know that until my little *unfortunate incident*, it was a certainty that I would be reelected."

He didn't seem to need my input and I didn't want to encourage him, so I didn't say anything.

"Even now, there is a chance I will win, because people really don't pay much attention to the races toward the end of the ballot."

"This really doesn't have anything to do with me," I said. "Deb is my friend, but I do what she tells me to do. I'm more like an office assistant."

He brushed away my objection like it was a fly. "I don't need you to do much," he said. "What I need is simple . . . just your eyes and ears and perhaps, your tongue."

That caused an involuntary shudder. This was starting to sound like a disgusting proposition. Whether it was a sexual one was still not clear to me. I started to object, but he continued to talk over me.

"No, no. I don't want you to be a spy. I have been around long enough that I know more than you can imagine of what is going on. It has come to my attention that Ms. Eubank has been the target of threats and intimidation."

"We kept all that out of the paper."

He waved a hand dismissively. "Young man, I don't get my information from the newspaper. The newspaper gets its information from me. I am aware of not only the fire, but the other incidents."

He looked at me shrewdly, measuring me. "What I don't know is how shaken Ms. Eubank is. I want to know if she is considering withdrawing."

I shook my head. "I don't know. But, if I did, I can't think of a reason why I would tell you." I really didn't like this man. I'm not one to be aggressive. Cutting remarks from a safe distance is more my style, but something about the sheer gall of having me picked up by a sheriff and grilled pissed me off enough to stiffen my spine. "You know I'm going to tell her about this conversation, right?"

"That would be an unfortunate act on your part. Of course you may, but . . .. Well, let me put it this way. You have heard that there are two ways to encourage a mule to work harder. One is to use a carrot. Another is to use a stick." He drew himself up, looking his most evil judge best. "I'm not a good one for choices. I believe in using both."

I began to stand. It was time to leave.

He half rose and held up placating hands. "Just a moment more. Please. I won't ask you to violate your conscience or your morals." He smiled as if the idea of me having a conscience or morals was amusing. "Just hear me out. Then I will have Officer Jenkins take you home. If you decide you want to, I will have no objection to your informing Ms. Eubank of our conversation, as long as you remember my view of encouraging a mule." Again, the smile that was reminiscent of the biblical snake in Eden.

“Not that I am comparing you to a mule.”

I drew a breath, torn between wanting to get far, far away and wondering what he could possibly want from me. Curiosity got the better of me and I sat.

"Good. Now, as I said, I don't want to know the ins and outs of the campaign. I really don't care. My only wish is that if Ms. Eubank decides to withdraw from the race, I am given advance notice. Timing may be of the essence and even a few hours may make a difference." He pulled a pad of paper toward himself, scribbled a number, then handed it to me. "If she makes that decision, and you call this number and inform whoever answers, I will make it worth your while. *Very* worth your while."

"What do you mean?"

"I am not a poor man. I have many assets and I can be generous. I have many friends who can also be generous. In addition to being generous, they often have reason to employ a bright young man. You certainly can do better than a low-level job at a university library with a boss who is both pedantic and unappreciative."

That scared me. The man knew where I worked and who I worked for and what Dustyn was like. This was some pretty deep knowledge, and I knew he was telling me so I understood the depth of his reach. His beady eyes drilled into me and he nodded.

"As I said, I can be quite generous, but I believe in both the carrot and the stick. Jobs and funding are so mercurial these days. Jobs can be here one day and gone the next. If Ms. Eubank were to make a decision and I had to wait to read about it in the newspaper, I would not be happy."

I do not react well to threats. However, I am also, at my core, a rather fearful being. I know when I am dealing with powers far greater than my own, and this guy was definitely above my pay grade. I didn't say anything. The judge stood.

"Well, this has been most refreshing. I am glad we could have a little chat. See yourself out. Officer Jenkins will take you home."

He sat, turned on the television, and ignored me.

I stood there a minute, then turned and left.

Officer Jenkins took me home and stopped in front of my house, not saying a word. I got out and he drove off.

I went inside, picked up the phone, and called Roger. I relayed all that had just happened.

"Gee, BB. I'm impressed. You got through all that and didn't puke or cry."

"Thanks for the vote of confidence. I did just fine, but now I have a nasty judge after me."

"Not to worry. It wasn't quite a confession, but it sure sounds like he wants to know when the scare tactics work so he can pull his goons off once Deb caves."

"But she's not going to cave."

"You know that and I know that, but he doesn't. You relax, BB. You've had a busy day. I'll call Nacho and delay our meeting. Come to the *Café* about six."

"But what if he comes after me? I *did* tell you he kept talking about sticks."

"Poor baby. I won't let anything happen to you. Who'd I make fun of if you got damaged? Don't worry. Both Nacho and I have taken on much bigger fish in the past than the judge. Fix yourself a drink and take a warm bath and you'll be fine. Then head over to Nacho's. Don't answer the door or the phone unless it's me or Nacho. Oh, and I think you'd better not tell Deb for now. If you do, she'll march right over to confront the judge. I don't want to try to stop a charging Deb."

"But—"

"No, BB. DBR. Drink. Bath. Relax. I'll call you later."

He hung up. I thought about it and couldn't come up with any better ideas, so I grabbed a drink, drew a bath, and applied myself to both.

Chapter Sixteen
Thursday Evening

"I won't cancel," Deb said. "It's Halloween and four days before the election. TiaRa has done me a great favor by inviting me. It's on all the posters. What kind of message will that send if I don't show?"

"If you get your pretty little ass blown off, what message will *that* send?" Nacho grumped.

"I can't believe anyone would go to such extremes," Deb said.

"It's possible," Roger said. "I've been digging into our favorite real estate tycoon, BurntHam. You know he's done some shady deals before."

Deb snorted. "I've sued him plenty of times because of it. When he tore down those houses that were slated for historic preservation so he could build student lofts, we almost had him. But it went before Judge Hawthorne. His rulings tanked the case."

"You think he bribed the judge?" Beau asked. "Isn't that illegal?"

Deb reached over and pinched his cheek. "You are so sweet and innocent, Beau. Don't ever change." She looked at the rest of us. "Nothing I can prove, but there was no reason for that case to go south and there have been others. That's one of the reasons I decided to run."

We had already discussed my meeting with the judge. Roger had been correct. Deb had wanted to run right over to the judge's house and attack. She was not a happy camper having to stay in a safe house and not go out campaigning. Nacho and Roger had talked her out of confronting the judge, but when they suggested she cancel tomorrow night's appearance at *Hoosier Daddy's* Halloween show, she became an immovable object.

"I won't cancel," Deb said. "It's Halloween and four days before the election. TiaRa has done me a great favor by inviting me. It's on all the posters. What kind of message will that send if I don't show?"

"If you get your pretty little ass blown off, what message will *that* send?" Nacho grumped.

"I can't believe anyone would go to such extremes," Deb said.

“It's possible," Roger said. "I've been digging into our favorite real estate tycoon, BurntHam. You know he's done some shady deals before."

Deb snorted. “I've sued him plenty of times because of it. When he tore down those houses that were slated for historic preservation so he could build student lofts, we almost had him. But it went before Judge Hawthorne. His rulings tanked the case."

"You think he bribed the judge?" Beau asked. "Isn't that illegal?"

Deb reached over and pinched his cheek. "You are so sweet and innocent, Beau. Don't ever change." She looked at the rest of us. "Nothing I can prove, but there was no reason for that case to go south and there have been others. That's one of the reasons I decided to run."

We had already discussed my meeting with the judge. Roger had been correct. Deb had wanted to run right over to the judge's house and attack. She was not a happy camper having to stay in a safe house and not go out campaigning. Nacho and Roger had talked her out of confronting the judge, but when they suggested she cancel tomorrow night's appearance at *Hoosier Daddy's* Halloween show, she became an immovable object.
I had seen her like this before. It would be easier t rearrange the faces on Mount Rushmore than to get her to change her mind. She was going to be at that show, even if it meant catching a bullet.

"BurntHam is desperate. The lake development is the biggest thing he's ever tried. All his businesses are tied up in it. He's borrowed against everything. If anything stops it or even delays it, he'll lose everything, and he is not a man who goes down without a fight. He has lots of bad guys as friends. He's used them before. He doesn't like you anyway. He doesn't like fags, so if some other people get hurt, he doesn't care. You really need to—"

"I really need to stand up and show these shitheads that they can't scare me," Deb snapped. "I won't cancel. I won't."

Roger sighed. "In a crowd like that, I don't know how we can keep you safe." He looked at Nacho. "Any more of your friends arrive?"

Nacho nodded. "Another seven got in today. We'll have nearly twenty scattered throughout the place. They can look for trouble and I'll have a few that can hurt anyone who tries anything. I don't want anyone to get hurt. Not Deb. Not anyone."

Deb nodded. "Focus on protecting everyone else. I don't mind risking my neck, but we've got to protect the crowd."

Nacho and Roger nodded.

A very unpleasant thought popped into my head. I tried to chase it away, but it wouldn't go. I felt sick. My mouth moved, but words refused to come out. Roger noticed.

"Working on your fish imitation, BB?" he asked with a smile.

My eyes kept getting wider. It had occurred to me that while Nacho's people would be watching and protecting the crowd and Deb, I would also be on the stage. I could picture the stage and see a clear image of how many bulletproof obstacles would *not* be standing between me and a psycho. I could see how many safe places would *not* be available to hide behind if someone started shooting. It was self- indulgent. It was petty. But I suddenly had a real desire not to be an innocent bystander. But it was so selfish. I could not get the words to come out, and I could not make the fear go away. Everyone was staring and I couldn't seem to climb far enough out of my growing whirlpool of terror to spit out words.

Finally Nacho smacked my leg. "Speak. Now. You look like you're about to barf and I don't want to put on a new muumuu."

The possibility of appearing petty bowed to the certainty of incurring Nacho's displeasure. Words finally spilled out. "If we are on stage, your people in the audience won't be able to help. They'll be able to see, but they'll be below us. They can't stop anything from happening. We'll be perched there like . . . like..." Words failed me.

Roger and Nacho looked at each other, considering. Suddenly Beau had an inspiration. "I know. Tia! It's her show. She can be up there during Deb's speech. She can do a repeat performance of the dancing judges."

Roger shook his head. "No. First time it took everyone by surprise. Try it again and it will be obvious that Deb is standing still in the middle of the dancing queens."

"Besides," Nacho said, "we need to have someone up there who knows what to do if something goes down. BB will be about as useful as a match in a windstorm."

A tickle of ego urged me to protest, but I agreed completely. I kept my mouth shut.

"I can't hide behind a bodyguard," Deb said. "How can I say I'll fight for the people when I'm hiding? I have to be there, front and center."

"We need to fill the stage with movement," Beau said. "So much movement that people can't track who is who. Everyone needs to blend into a kaleidoscope of color."

Nacho stared at him. "Good copy for an ad, Beau, but ain't so helpful in real life."

Beau was on a roll. He had an idea and he was not to be stopped. "It's more than an ad, Nacho. Think about it. When you see a line of chorus girls, you can't pick out one from the rest, can you?"

"Cream puff, look at me. How much time do you think I've ever spent watching chorus girls?"

Beau rolled his eyes. "Imagine it."

Aunt May spoke up, "It is true that a cluster of females wearing the same outfits do tend to blend. I remember when I was a debutante. A whole group of us had a coming out affair."

I looked at Roger, who was about to make a lewd comment and shook my head. May's story was sure to be more interesting than a tired coming out pun.

"When we were presented at the Flower of the South cotillion, we were all bedecked in such similar gowns, it was difficult to distinguish between the girls, particularly in low light. I had arranged to meet Warfield Alexander in the upstairs linen closet and quite unbeknownst to either of us, Lavinia Siebert had set up a similar parlay with Adolphus Ringholt and when I arrived"

"Aunt May, while I dearly love your historical reflections," Beau interrupted, "I was building to a certain climax." He looked at Roger, again halting an untoward remark. "As it were."

"Oh, my dear, I am most sorry. Please do continue. I shall regale you with my adventure in the linen closet another time."

I was tempted to ask her to continue. Aunt May's stories were always more entertaining and often more useful than Beau's stories, but events were more pressing.

"The answer is obvious," Beau continued. "We need to cast aside the robes and go with gowns." He was so wrapped up in his vision, he stood and twirled as if splendidly attired. "And Deb and Petunia need to be as glamorous as the girls. Instead of hiding the queens in robes, we'll hide the judge in gowns!" He plopped back down, awash in the fantasy that played before his eyes.

I looked at Deb. Her mouth was moving, but no words came out. Then I caught sight of Petunia. Now, Petunia resembles a stone gargoyle in appearance and temperament. I always was careful around Petunia. Like a gorilla or an elephant, she was not intentionally destructive without reason, but if one was to startle her or, being even more foolhardy, irritate her, the resulting carnage was a predestined consequence. After Beau's suggestion, Petunia had become more still than usual, as if even breath had stopped. Her face was turning interesting and dangerous shades of red and her entire being swelled. An explosion was imminent, but not one that would deliver pieces of Petunia over those gathered. No, the pieces would be parts of Beau and anyone unfortunate enough to be close by.

I instinctively shut my eyes and ducked my head. I knew it would not protect me, but, like a child pulling the covers over his head, it was all I could think of to do to ward off the monsters. Thankfully, some of us were not as clueless as Beau nor as helpless as I. Nacho stepped forward, into Petunia's field of vision and pointed toward the door. "Why don't you take a look around the perimeter while Roger and I slap around some sense. I'd let you in on the fun, but blood is hard to clean up and these chairs are worth something, even if who's sittin' in em ain't." Petunia blinked. The bulking unbulked a bit. She glanced at Roger, who nodded. Then she sighed, rolled her shoulders, and headed out the door.

I uncovered my head and unclenched my sphincter.

Beau let out a little yelp of protest. Dear Beau had no idea that his life had just been spared when the headman's ax was a hairbreadth away. "Wait! I know exactly what to do." Petunia didn't stop. Beau turned his attention to Deb. "Well, that means we have more time to work on you." His eyes swiveled toward me. "And BB. Your trusty right-hand man should be right up there with you."

I suddenly understood Deb's choking reaction. I found it hard to draw a breath. I have nothing against women—I'd let my sister marry one. But to dress like one? It is not a moral judgment; it is an aesthetic one. I have tried before and all the pushing, padding, prodding, perfume, and powder in the world cannot transform me into a butterfly. Well, perhaps the Western Bean Cutworm moth, a hairy, rotted leaf with wings, known to destroy corn crops, but not a butterfly.

"I can't do it," Deb said. "I don't mean I won't. I mean I can't. I haven't worn anything more glamorous than a business suit since I was in my teens. I even got married in shorts and a tank top."

I looked stunned. She shrugged. "It was Hawaii. We were both pretty drunk. It was kind of spur of the moment."

"Marry in haste. Repent in leisure," Roger said.

"You got it. But back to the point. I don't have a dress. I don't have heels. Even if I did, I couldn't pull off looking anywhere near as good as the girls in the show, and I can't walk two steps in heels."

"The outfit is no problem," Beau said. "With the queens in town, there will be glamour galore in any and every size. For shoes, the only problem may be finding a pair that are small enough for your dainty feet."

"You aren't listening, Beau. I can't walk in heels. I also can't walk right. I walk like a dyke lawyer, which is what I am. I'm happy with who I am, but I can't do dress-up."

Beau was having none of it. "Tia can teach you. She can teach anyone. She can teach Petunia, too."

"Nope," Roger said, "not Petunia. You know that the people who had religion shoved down their throats when they were kids have the biggest problem with religion. Well, Petunia's caring parents tried to beat the butch out of her. When she was five, she told her parents she wanted to be a cowboy for Halloween. They beat her and bought her a princess costume. She shredded it and refused to go trick or treating. She's never gone to another Halloween celebration. It's only because she cares so much for you, Deb, that she is coming tomorrow. But she will *not* be dressing as a girl."

He looked around the table. "And if any of you, BB . . . Beau, ever even hint to Petunia that you know this, I will do such horrible things to you, you will never recover." He stared at us, impassive as a hangman. "Do you understand?"

We nodded. The calm stillness of his gaze was more chilling than anything I could imagine.

Nacho spoke up, "What about as a dude?" "What do you mean?" Roger asked.

"A lot of the girls have a stud muffin to lean on when they come out on stage. They don't do anything but stand there and flex. Petunia can flex with the best of them."

“That might work," Roger said slowly.

“We'd just have to find a tux or at least a suit," Beau said. "Oh, and she should wear dark sunglasses. It will be a great look, plus she'll be able to see even with all the lights on stage."

Roger nodded. “I'll talk to her, but I think she'll go for it."

"I'll call Foxy," I said. "If he doesn't have a tux that will fit her, I bet Suave does." Suave, Foxy's amour, was an inveterate collector of all things vintage and lovely. I was pretty sure she would have a rack of vintage suits somewhere in the inner reaches of *Suave Delights*, her antique store which was more a place for her to keep her collections than a thriving retail operation.

"All right," Nacho said, "we meet back here tomorrow afternoon to work out the details and give Deb a chance to learn how to girl it up. Hopefully there won't be any more surprises between now and then. That's all the planning for tonight. I've got a business to run and those nachos ain't gonna make themselves."

With that, Nacho stood and went back to the kitchen. Roger also stood. "I've got to talk to Petunia and make sure she's still willing." He went through the doors that led to *Hoosier Daddy*, heading for the street.

Beau, Aunt May, and I looked at each other.

"I believe," Aunt May murmured, "that a few drinks may be in order."

She didn't state a purpose, but truth be told, when did we ever need a reason to have a few? They would go nicely with the story of Aunt May and the linen closet.

Chapter Seventeen
Glamour Unleashed

The next afternoon found us back at *Hoosier Daddy* in the big back room, ass deep in outfits. TiaRa kept a large assortment of glamour for the big and broad in the dressing rooms. Adding to that collection, Suave had brought a rack of clothes and an enormous box of shoes from *Suave Delights*. It had taken Foxy numerous trips to bring everything in. Several of the performers scheduled for that evening's show had volunteered to appear with Deb. They flocked around the treasures from Suave, oohing and chattering until TiaRa sent them out to the patio so she could work alone with Deb and me.

Petunia was not present. Roger assured us that she had grudgingly agreed to give up her black T- shirt, jeans, and combat boots for a suit, but she had absolutely refused to take part in the afternoon's exercise.

"She said she might get irked and if that happened, she would not take responsibility for her actions," Roger said.

I had never seen Petunia when she didn't seem at the very least irked. If what I had experienced was her unirked, I didn't want to witness what irked looked like.

"I trust you explained that if she did not agree to a fitting, the suit may not drape correctly," Foxy said.

"I'm sure she wouldn't bitch if you wrapped the damn thing around her and stapled it into place, as long as she don't have to show up," Nacho said.

"You know . . ." I began, edging away.

"Not a chance, BB," Nacho snapped. "You gotta pretty yourself up and you're gonna need a lot of help. Even I don't want to upset Petunia, but you, I got no problem with."

"If I can stand it, you can stand it," Deb said, coming in from the dressing room, TiaRa following behind, tucking in errant baubles. Deb was attired in a gown that had survived the Roaring Twenties. It dripped scarves and fringe in an array of colors from royal-blue to sea-green. With each step, the fabric moved like aspen leaves in a slight breeze, flashing silver underlays before settling back to the full rich color. The effect was stunning – Mae West and Claudette Colbert would have torn each other (but not the dress) to shreds for the chance to wear it. The tailoring was exquisite, emphasizing her figure, showing off curves I didn't know she had and softening her visage. Instead of giving her usual impression—that of a block of limestone falling toward you, so you better step aside, she was someone who drew your eye, who you wanted to look at, who you wanted to know. She looked . . . well, she looked like a man in a dress, but a very elegant man in a very elegant dress. She looked, dare I say, glamorous.

Beau let out a whistle. "Divine," he said in a throaty whisper.

"The state of being or the dear departed actor?" Deb asked with a smile. "In either case, thank you." She walked to the chair where Slasher was sleeping, picked up the little dog, who sniffed her suspiciously, then gave her a little lick and sat down. "Your turn, BB. Wow me."

I sighed and, fighting back the urge to run, went back to the dressing room with TiaRa. First, she handed me a star-spangled mini. "I might cut myself on one of the bangles," I protested. I'll look like a cheap whore."

"You have no reason to fear on that account," Tia said. "While I do love you, BB, I doubt anyone would ever imagine you were selling your body for money." When I began to protest, she held up her hand. "In this world, some are sellers and others must be buyers, and both are necessary."

I struggled into the scrap of fabric, not daring to look in the mirror. Tia looked appraisingly at me and cocked her head. "It *does* give you freedom of movement. However, you must absolutely remember to keep your legs together at all times. Otherwise, well, there might be complaints. Let us see what the others think."

TiaRa led the way, nearly pulling me. I stepped into the light and was met by gasps from all concerned. Roger made retching noises. Beau tittered and shook his head. Deb bent to pat Slasher, but I could see her shoulders shaking as a hidden laugh bubbled through her.

"No chance," Nacho said. "Remember, I sell food here. He comes out in that outfit and nobody is gonna be able to get anything down, and anything that has already gone down is gonna come back up."

"Plus, we'll have to deal with all the cases of hysterical blindness," Roger said.

Even Aunt May seemed a little shocked. "Perhaps something with a bit more length. You have so many sterling qualities, BB. However, I must admit that 'come hither legs' is not one of them. You put me in mind of Carlotta Clements. We girls used to call her Clip Clop Clements because of her rather horsey face. Her legs resembled nothing so much as extremely large sausage casings, but she did have the most melodic of voices and the things she could do with her throat kept a cadre of young men quite interested in spending time with her—provided she was properly attired in long skirts so as not to distract."

I turned and ran back to the dressing room. TiaRa followed close behind. I ripped off the mini and reached for my pants.

"We'll try something else," Tia said.

"No. I'm done," I said. "This body was not made to wear a dress."

Tia grabbed my ear and twisted. It hurt. She got very close to me and spoke emphatically. I had never heard TiaRa shout, but I was learning how she managed to keep a passel of drag queens in line every Sunday evening for her *Parade of Gowns* show. "Listen to me, BB. It is not what you have, but how you present it. I have seen performers uglier than you," she looked me up and down, "much, much uglier than you, who were able to sparkle on stage and keep a crowd enthralled because they did not allow the crowd to wallow in the unpleasant lines. No, they learned to project the sparkle, the joy, the glamour that lies within. This world is full of ugliness. Ugliness is easy to see. The challenge to which we must bend our every effort is to discover that little grain of beauty and celebrate it until that is all we and everyone else experiences. And it is not just for you that you must undertake this challenge. It is for Deb. For if you fail, she will be out there on her own, without you to support or protect her if she needs you, and then how shall you feel? Who shall you be?"

TiaRa let go of my ear and stepped back, allowing me to decide if I was going to put on my pants and walk out or put on my big boy panties and try another dress.

I sighed. "Perhaps an ankle-length, but with a slit so it's easier to walk," I suggested.

Tia smiled and nodded. "I have just the thing." She dug through a rack of bejeweled outfits. She came back with a floor-length sheath, looking vaguely like a 60's Hollywood impression of an Asian hostess.

It was relatively plain, made of bright red satin that shimmied when I walked. Black braided cords swirled in patterns along crucial areas of bulge, if not hiding, at least distracting the eye. A long slit ran up the side, allowing me to walk without much restriction. As I looked in the mirror, TiaRa came up behind me and put a tall, black wig on my head. Then she turned me and applied some powder and eyeliner, giving my eyes a vaguely Asian shape. The overall effect wasn't dazzling, but I had not hoped for dazzling. I might believe in fairies, but miracles are another thing. I was not painful to look at and that was enough. TiaRa applauded.

"You are stunning. Absolutely stunning. Now go out there and wow those doubters."

I threw my head back, stuck my padded chest out and strode into the spotlight, took a turn, and curtsied low.

Unfortunately, as I curtsied low, the slit tore open, exposing far more thigh than I would want to show to anyone except in low light situations fueled by an over-abundance of alcohol and lust.

A collective horrified cry, followed by individual moans, shredded my new-found confidence. I struggled back into a standing crouch, turned, and fled back to the dressing room.

Tia was waiting. She held up a hand. "One more try, dear. Just one more and we'll have it. Do not despair. Auntie Tia has the answer." She pulled out an enormous pile of electric chartreuse tulle wrapped around some hideous shiny fabric. I'm sure my eyes widened at the sight. "I got eight of them at once," she said. "I was leaving Reno after a brief, but taxing engagement and these treasures were piled in a heap outside a dusty little thrift store. The proprietress thought they had been bridesmaid dresses and was willing to accept any offer as the shop was small and the dresses, as you can see, are not. I've been saving them for a dance number, but I think unveiling one, particularly on Halloween, is appropriate. I realize it is just this side of horrendous, but it will cover any and all unsightly bulges. It is floor-length, yet should allow you enough freedom of movement to keep up with Deb. And even better " She held up a pair of chartreuse, patent leather pumps with three-inch heels that were large enough for a clown and, unfortunately, looked to be my size. "There are matching shoes."

I wanted to protest. I wanted to do something, anything to get out of there, but there stood TiaRa, sweet and delicate, but as unyielding as time. And on stage was Deb, already in a dress I am quite sure she hated, but willing to do what needed to be done to answer the call. Who was I to weenie out? I sighed and reached for the dress. To my dismay, it fit. TiaRa handed me the shoes.

“Don't put them on yet. Let's go out to the stage and I will teach you and Deb to walk in heels. But first, I will chase away that rabble. You do not need a mocking crowd, at least not now. There will be time enough for that tonight."

When I began to protest, she held up a hand.

"Tonight, the lights will be flashing. The music will be blasting. The liquor will be flowing. The crowd will be much more interested in each other and themselves than you. All you need do is enter and shadow Deb, watching out for anything untoward. You will be a sensation."

I knew better than to protest. She had commanded, so I reluctantly followed her out to the stage. With a few words, she sent the others out the doors to *Nacho Mama's Patio Café*, leaving only me and Deb on stage. Deb clutched Slasher and both gave TiaRa the hairy eyeball, obviously wishing even more than me that we were all somewhere else. But TiaRa was not to be deterred. "Put on your pumps, my dears. It is time to learn to glide."

Deb and I looked at each other, shared a sigh, and reached for the objects of our despair. Deb put Slasher down and put on her pumps, which were iridescent blue, shimmering to silver. They also had three-inch heels, but Deb's were not the stiletto fuck me pumps TiaRa had foisted on me. Deb stood and took a tentative step and then another. She nodded to herself and began clumping around the stage. "Hey, this isn't as hard as I thought. Must be like riding a bike. It all comes back to me."

Tia gave a small cough. "Deb, dear, you are to be congratulated for not falling. However, you are walking . . . how shall I put this? Well, you put me in mind of your usual footwear."

"I usually wear SAS when I dress up and work boots for around the house. They give the best support."

Tia nodded. "The second one. You are wearing those lovely slippers like they are combat boots, which is an impressive feat, given how delicate they are."

Deb opened her mouth to protest, but TiaRa kept talking over her, something most prosecutors were unable to accomplish. "You must glide, my dear. *Glide*. Imagine a line stretching out to heaven before you and place each toe on that line. Step forward, not to the side. Reach your toe to that line, for maximum glamour. Lift your head, throw back your shoulders, and point to the line with your toe."

Deb sighed and tried.

TiaRa applauded. "Better. Much better. Now, do not give in to that temptation to look down at your feet. You are a princess. Your feet will do as you command. Look up at your subjects, bestowing your grace upon them. Now again. Glide around the stage."

Deb concentrated and after a few stumbles, was soon doing a passable impression of a glide. Maybe this wasn't going to be so hard. I shoved my feet into the chartreuse pumps that came with the monstrosity of a dress I wore. I had a brief image of the poor bridesmaid who had worn this punishment, sobbing as she considered the humiliation of appearing so bedecked with the additional pain of knowing that there would be photographic evidence to forever remind her of this horror—which would certainly last longer than the marriage it claimed to celebrate. My lot was much less painful than hers, so I resolved to make the best of it. TiaRa beckoned and I stood.

Immediately, my ankles buckled and I dropped like a sack of tulle-frosted rocks. I didn't think I broke anything internally except any tattered remnants of my pride. With hope, I checked the shoes for damage. Damn. They were unscathed. I grabbed the chair for support and slowly pulled myself up. Wobbling dangerously, I turned to face Tia.

She nodded encouragement. "Very good, BB. Now, try a step. Keep the steps very short. Focus on your ankles. Try to keep them from twisting."

"I thought you said to think about walking a line."

"That was for Deb. For you, I believe we should concentrate on keeping you upright. Gliding will be a secondary goal."

I nodded. I steadied myself, took a breath, and aimed for Deb's chair, which was a few feet away. As graceful as a drunken giraffe on a skateboard, I stumbled forward. Slasher saw me coming and with a yelp, ran away. TiaRa reached out to steady me, but my weight and momentum were too much for her slim form. She stepped back and allowed me to crash to the floor. I lay there, wondering if there was any real reason to get up. I heard Roger laugh. Evidently, he had come back in and had seen my demonstration of the power of gravity.

"Now I know why they call you Grace behind your back," he said.

TiaRa put her hands on her hips. "I banished you for a reason, Roger. This is difficult enough without your mocking. BB is struggling in order to help Deb, not to amuse you. I will ask you again to leave and let us get on with it."

Roger came up to the stage. "While I enjoyed the show, I actually did come in to help. BB, pry those shoes off your feet and toss them over here."

I didn't ask why. I didn't really care. To have the implements of pain and humiliation banished from my feet was reward enough. I did as he asked.

Roger revealed that he held in his hand a battery powered saw. "Nacho keeps some tools in the office, just in case something needs a quick fix on the patio." He took a shoe and sliced the heel in half. He repeated the process with the other shoe and tossed both back to me. "The taller the shoe, the more difficult they are to stand and walk in," he said. "Try 'em now. You might be able to get around without a walker."

I pulled the shoes back on, although my feet protested. Then, I slowly pulled myself up. I did not immediately collapse. That seemed promising. I took a step. Then another. I was not steady. I was certainly not gliding or floating, but I was not falling, either. I took a few steps. I was constantly on the verge of a fall, but I managed to stay upright.

Tia hurried to Roger and gave him a quick peck on the cheek. "You are a genius! I am sure with some practice BB will be able to pull this off." She cast an appraising eye at my continued attempts to walk.

"I believe we shall have you enter and then simply walk to the front of the stage and shimmy a bit. Just stand and shimmy. That will provide you a good view of the crowd and will not risk calling attention. It is an unpleasant showstopper when one of the girls takes a header on stage during a number."

She looked at Deb and I practicing our walking. "A bit more practice and I shall declare you both ready. Then we shall have all the girls come in and we will run through the choreography. I promise to keep it simple. We want flashy, but not difficult."

"Nacho has a spread out on the patio," Roger said. "Once you're finished here, come on out and let us laugh at you before the doors open."

"Absolutely not," TiaRa said. "After rehearsal, you will both go back to the dressing rooms and change. I will not allow you to spill things on your gowns, and it is a law of nature that beautiful garments attract all food and drink within easy reach."

"Then BB's dress should be safe," Roger said. "That is, without a doubt, the ugliest thing I have ever seen, the recent flashes of your thighs excluded."

Tia turned him toward the doors. "Goodbye, Roger. When we are finished and changed, we shall join you on the patio. For now, we have work to do and you must have more important business elsewhere."

Roger did not follow orders often. However, what Tia decreed was not to be ignored. He saluted and left. Tia raised her voice, calling to the girls who had been gossiping out on the patio. "Dumplings! It is time. Our babies have been broken in, but you must watch out for them. Let us give it a run through, and then we shall eat and drink and prepare for the Halloween delights."

I sighed. Unbidden a line from *Scrooged,* that great Bill Murray film written by Glazer and O'Donoghue, popped into my head. "Break a leg everybody. I feel really weird about tonight."

Chapter Eighteen
The Halloween Show

It was a wild night. *Hoosier Daddy* was full to the tits with every kind of everyone. Even straight people understand that Halloween beats and gyrates closest to the hearts of the gayity. Straight girls tend to use the holiday to dress as sluts. Straight guys who have been working on and admiring their bodies so much it is obvious they wish they could fuck themselves if it wasn't so gay, try to expose as much of their efforts as possible, while those who don't have the body beautiful go for weird. Gays run the spectrum from odd to just plain wrong to amazing. Wherever they land, they are fabulous. I generally don't even try. I enjoy being a spectator. I recognize and appreciate professionals in all professions, and those who spend months in planning and preparation deserve my adulation and they get it. Everyone who was anyone or even knew anyone who was anyone was at *Hoosier Daddy* that night. I huddled backstage. I do not enjoy being the center of attention or even on the periphery of attention. I do not enjoy being in dangerous situations. Yet, far too soon I was going to parade my middle-aged ass onto the stage in an unapologetically chartreuse dress and heels that, despite being trimmed by Roger, were still far too high for me to handle. I was going to be on that stage while an unknown number of assassins owing allegiance to an unknown person might or might not attempt to rain destruction down upon the stage in general and Deb in particular. And I would be standing a bit in front of Deb. This would place me between the potential assassins and her, albeit I'd be a bit to the side, when she stepped out of the crowdof queens, revealed herself, and spoke. This was a job for a hero. When I was a child and we played superheroes, I was never the superhero. Occasionally, I would muster up my macho and be the trusty sidekick. More often, I was the damsel in distress or one in the crowd who got to say, "Look, up in the sky. Here he comes." I was fine with that. What was going on this evening was not something I had always dreamed of. I sat in the dressing room, trying not to barf.

Roger came in and handed me a drink. I shook my head. My stomach was already trying to squeeze itself dry. He pushed it at me again. "Drink it, BB. You need it." Roger liked to push my buttons, but he had been a friend for a lot of years. He was always there when the world and the people in it had decided it was time to play 'let's fuck with BB'. I grabbed the drink and took a big gulp. It did not magically make me feel better, but I became slightly less interested in laughing at the floor. Roger sat down and put a hand on my knee, giving me a friendly squeeze.

"Let me give you the lay of the land. Some of it is scary, but I'm sure you are imagining much worse. We are not going to be attacked by a swarm of commandos. There are no killer aliens out there. We have a couple of very butch, very experienced guards at the door. They are checking everyone coming through and they are not being subtle about it. There will be no bazookas or grenade launchers getting in. Nacho has Twinks scattered all over the place. Some are waiters. Some are in costume. All are being very friendly and rubbing up against anyone who looks suspicious so they can frisk them for any weapons that might have evaded detection. That's the good news."

I relaxed. The combination of reassuring words, a very strong cocktail, and Roger's confidence was working. I was relaxed enough to ask the question I had been avoiding. "And the bad news?"

Roger grimaced. "Well, there is some uncertainty. We know that Felcher is no longer a worry. Besides, he and his followers are having a rally to exorcise the demons brought to Earth by this holiday at the town square. We believe Judge Hawthorne is at home drinking. That's how he usually spends his Friday evenings. We called earlier and he was home and already slurring. However, we've been watching BurntHam, and something is up there. He was at his real estate office earlier. He managed to sneak out at some point during the day, because just before the office closed, we went in and no one had seen him for hours. We've checked his house and the motel where he usually goes when he's screwing some new squeeze and doesn't want his wife to know. We couldn't find him. So, he got away and is still gone. It's late and he should be home by now, so he's up to something and with him, you can bet it's not something nice. So, pay attention when you are up there, BB. Don't worry about the choreography or the other dancers. Get up to the front of the stage and keep scanning the audience. If you see anything, wave and point. Nacho's Twinks will be in the crowd and will take care of it." Roger slapped me on back. "You'll be fine, BB. Just go out there and sparkle, Neeley, sparkle."

I looked up, wanting to know more. A flash went off. The bastard had taken a picture of me, capturing my worried expression atop this hideous chartreuse dress. He smiled. "Will you be wanting this as an eight-by-ten or poster size?"

I would have thrown the glass at him, but it was plastic and wouldn't have done any damage or provided a satisfying crash. Roger was saved from the passel of profanities I was stringing together by the entrance of Deb. She looked completely at ease in her dress and was gliding across the floor like she had been wearing heels all her life. It takes a big man not to be jealous of such dexterity. I am not a big man. I thought evil thoughts toward both of them as I struggled to stand. Deb caught me before I pitched forward onto the floor.

"Easy there, BB. We can't have you hurting yourself before the big number. Euphillia is finishing her set. Then TiaRa is going to sing *Goodbye December* to calm the crowd down a bit. Then we hit the stage as she sings *Do You*. All you have to do is make it from the back of the stage to the front without falling. During my speech, which I promise will be short, Thumper will play *47 Bus* quietly, just to keep some sound going in the background. Stand at the front of the stage and move to the music. Not too much or you'll fall off your heels. Watch the crowd. If you see anything weird . . .." She paused, realizing she had just asked me to point out anything weird in a gay bar on Halloween night. She smiled. "Well, if you see anyone who looks like they may be planning to take me out, wave at one of Nacho's Twinks. Then duck and cover." She looked at me and squeezed my arm. "Probably nothing will happen. This is just being careful. Try to have some fun." She grinned. "You do have one of the best seats in the house. You'll be able to see all the costumes."

At that point, a group of the girls swarmed into the room, checking their makeup. Even above their chatter, I could hear TiaRa sing the sensuous song of love slipped away.

"I am detaching my broken heart from you
My broken heart can now wander the world free of you
What a funny picture we drew Shove it in a frame
We're through
Goodbye December,
Hello New Year. Goodbye . . ."

Then a roar of applause. Someone clapped their hands and called out, "This is it. Let's get out there and show these bitches how it is done!"

Thumper's pounding rhythm began, ushering in *Do You*, a delightfully filthy and fun song.

The girls hit the stage running, jumping, and dancing. I followed, staggering in the heels, focusing my entire being on not taking a plunge to the floor. Suddenly, I saw the edge of the stage loom before me. I had made it. Saint Lance had watched over me and guided me safely to my destination. I lurched to a stop. My forward momentum nearly drove me off the stage, but by windmilling my arms, I was able to stop just as TiaRa stopped singing. Thumper continued into an instrumental version of *47 Bus*, the music, soft and hypnotic. This was too wild a crowd on too weird a night to stop the drum beat or the bass line. Too many substances were pulsing through the bodies out there and they absolutely needed something to jerk and sway to, even if a speech was going on. Thumper, the musical conductor of feelings, merely slowed and quieted the throbbing in order to focus attention on what was said.

TiaRa gave a regal wave encompassing the crowd, which continued to bob and sway along with the music and the girls on stage. "I feel the moon tonight, don't you?" she cried.

The crowd roared in agreement.

"I know why they call them lunatics, don't you?" Again, the crowd roared back.

"And for we happy lunatics, we must celebrate ourselves and rejoice, and we do tonight!"

This bobbing along with the music was getting pretty easy. Maybe I had more coordination than I thought. I began to smile. This was actually kind of fun. I looked out at the crowd bursting with nearly naked boys in all kinds of décor. There were wonderful witches, one who outdid the Divine Bette, wig to the sky and all. There was a Marie Antoinette in full regalia and her partner, a perfect copy sans head. There was a huge bearded Tooth Fairy, in a pink tutu with a magic wand and wings. There were several hunks and hulks. It was a phantasm of sights. This was fun!

"And now, a lovely surprise for you. In our small backwater boondock, we are about to make history. We are about to elect a real live lesbian to be a judge. And it's about time, isn't it?"

The crowd went nuts. This was a group that had never been able to celebrate one of their own. Even through the intoxicants, the importance of getting out and helping to create history was getting through. I could see it. I could see the fire sparking to life in those eyes as I looked across the crowd.

Tia continued, "And I have an extra special bit of history just for you right here tonight. On this very stage, our first, our only judge-to-be is right here and for the first time ever, I present to you *in a dress*, Deborah Eubank."

Thumper raised the volume and pounded out the bass line as Deb strode forward out of the line of girls, looking absolutely fabulous. I turned to look, but the movement threw off my balance and I started to teeter, so I turned back to the crowd. Deb began to speak. She could only get a couple of words out at a time—the crowd was so excited that the cheering would stop her. She loved it and they loved her. She played the crowd like TiaRa did when she sang. I have no idea how performers do it, but I can feel it and appreciate it when they do. I concentrated on shaking my butt and arms to the music that had dropped into the background. I'm sure the other girls were doing much better at keeping up the excitement. I was just happy to keep upright. I looked across the crowd of smiling faces and felt good.

I noticed that the big, bearded Tooth Fairy had moved nearly in front of me. There is something wonderfully wrong about a big ol' hunka hunka in a pink tutu. I grinned at him. He didn't grin back. His attention was fixed on Deb. However, he was not smiling. He was just staring. Something in the back of my mind tickled. I started watching him more carefully. He was playing with his magic wand. It was about three feet long and trailed stars and strands of glitter. But he was pulling off the covering and it was looking less and less like a wand and more and more like a weapon.

Recalling what I had been told, I looked for Roger or Petunia or one of Nacho's Twinks. I couldn't see Roger. Petunia was at the back of the stage, guarding the way in. I saw a couple of cute Twinks, but didn't know if they were Nacho's boys or not. I started to raise my hand and kind of gesture toward the Tooth Fairy. I was trying to be cool and not alert him that I had noticed anything untoward. He continued to pull away the spangles. He was looking down at the wand and then up at Deb, and I could see a look of menace grow across his features. I waved my hands over my head and then pointed down at him. Some in the crowd saw what I was doing and waved, too. They thought it was a celebratory gesture. I began to wave my hands and point more emphatically. I nearly lost my balance, but no one seemed to get the message.

No one was heading in that direction. I looked at the man, who was no longer looking fairy-like at all. He had finished pulling all the detritus off his wand and while I was not a weapons guy, even I could recognize that what was once a wand was now, very obviously, a weapon. A blow gun. He reached into his bag and pulled out, not a handful of glitter, but a rather large dart with a very large and very sharp point. By this time, subtle was no longer on the table. I waved my hands wildly above my head, then pointed at the guy. I did not care if he saw. I had to stop him, and no one seemed to be coming to do anything about it. Deb was talking. The girls were dancing. And the Tooth Fairy dropped the dart into his blow gun.

I raised both hands above my head, waving wildly. I jumped into the air to get someone's attention. Bad move. I came down and my ankle buckled. Note to self—jumping in heels is a bad idea. I was falling. There was nothing I could do about it. The great defender of Deb was going to end up in a heap on the stage and create a nice diversion while the Tooth Fairy shot her with a blow gun and escaped in the ensuing riot.

But as I fell, Saint Lance again interceded. No, he did not keep me from falling, but he gave me a bit of a push and I plunged off the stage right on top of the Tooth Fairy.

He struggled to push me off. "Get off of me, you faggot," he growled. *Bad move on his part.*

When I fell, the music had stopped and the crowd went quiet. There are levels of quiet. There is the quiet when you step out at midnight after a snow storm and the new fallen snow muffles every sound. There is the quiet when the screaming baby finally cries itself to sleep and you sit back with a sigh. But the quiet that echos when a club full of wild partiers is suddenly struck dumb, leaves the ears ringing and gasping for more of what had been pummeling them.

It was into this quiet that the Tooth Fairy's growl burst. And the entire mass of people turned to see who was calling who a faggot in this, our own house.

He was quickly identified, and a pack of

professionals and volunteers swarmed him and escorted him ungently outside where Nacho and Roger pulled the man aside to see what he had to say. It was not going to be a pleasant conversation for him. I'm not sure what orifice the blow gun would end up in, but I don't think he'd be walking right for a while.

Petunia had swiftly thrown herself in front of Deb as I fell and was trying to pull her off stage. But Deb was having none of it. She stayed right there in the middle of the stage. She gestured to Thumper to begin to play again and for the girls to dance. And she stepped to the microphone and she said, "They have always tried to silence us. When that didn't work, they have tried to beat us and kill us. But we will not be stopped. We will go out and we will vote. And we will stand up proudly and proclaim who we are. And for those who do not want us, we say, 'then step away. Live your life, but we *will* live ours.' For we are here. We are queer. And damn it, we vote!"

And the crowd went wild. We all cheered and roared and cried because we could. A couple of very sweet, very cute boys helped me up and with a proud, total lack of grace, I climbed back on the stage.

TiaRa came forward and said, "And that is why we celebrate and sing." And she launched into *People Person.*

"So darling won't you be my valentine Let's go punting on the Serpentine
I'm in love with everybody all the time Starting with you.
You'll do fine!"

Deb and I headed off stage. Both Deb and Petunia had to help me a bit. I was bruised and battered from my fall and wouldn't be wearing heels any time soon. Hopefully not again in this lifetime. But the night was over, and we were all in one piece. And tomorrow was Saturday and I was allowed to sleep in. I planned to.

Chapter Nineteen
Saturday

In my youth I was quite the little politico. I would ring doorbells, stuff envelopes, and make phone calls with the most ardent supporters. I no longer do. It is not that I feel less strongly for and against candidates. It is that I have grown increasingly timid in my later years. I simply cannot bring myself to ring a stranger's doorbell to foist my desires upon them. Perhaps it is that I have grown increasingly bothered by others who take it upon themselves to try to convince me that their religion, politics, or siding is essential to my well-being. I remember when I was young, I was fascinated with how different people viewed the world. While I was advocating a specific person or position, I had no judgment if someone disagreed. I was more interested in how they had come to that conclusion. I am less fascinated now. I have asked enough people and seen enough ways of viewing the world and settled rather happily into my beliefs. I don't particularly want to change anyone else's beliefs, unless they specifically are a danger to myself or the world as a whole, and I don't welcome the opportunity to discuss religion, politics, alien abduction, or anything that hints of how the world goes around—at least not with random strangers who show up at my door and want to share or convince me that their particular viewpoint is the only right way to see the world.

Thankfully, there was a vibrant group of volunteers who did not share my reclusive nature and this was the last weekend before the election. They had and talking to people at the farmer's market, encouraging one and all to get to the polls on Tuesday and vote for Deb. Deb had been up since dawn and had been dropping in wherever people were gathered, shaking hands, answering questions, and cheering on the volunteers. She loved it. They loved her. And I loved the opportunity to sleep late. However, far earlier than I had hoped, my phone rang repeatedly with Nacho, then Roger, and finally Deb, all urging me to arise and greet the day, although not one of them phrased it so poetically.

"Get your ass out there and do some good," was the way Nacho put it.

"The fairy you fell on didn't talk, even after our best attempts at persuasion. We might have eventually gotten through, but someone called the cops and they rescued him by arresting the shit," reported Roger. "I'm still looking into BurntHam and the judge, so you need to keep an eye on Deb. It's all hands on deck. Don't make me call again or I'll send Petunia to get you."

Deb was much nicer, asking me to bring more flyers, drinks, and come pick up Slasher, who was getting tired. "Oh, and I forgot my briefcase at *Daddy's* last night. Nacho says it's there. Could you swing by and get it?"

There was no fighting the clamor. I got dressed and headed out. The day was full of errands, ferrying volunteers to new areas or the bathroom, bringing food and drink to those in the trenches, and trying to keep an eye on Deb. She could smell victory and she wasn't going to let anyone or anything stop her. I'm no psychic, but I couldn't see Judge Hawthorne winning unless he or BurntHam managed to kill her. And Petunia was with Deb at all times, so I felt pretty certain that wasn't going to happen. If I had to choose between a tank and Petunia to keep me safe, I'd go with Petunia. She has more mobility and more anger. I was also around to protect Deb, but compared to Petunia, I was as intimidating as a dollop of marshmallow fluff. We had to keep the defenses up. Deb absolutely refused to halt or even slow her exposure this weekend. These were the days to get people fired up, one voter at a time. The local Democratic Party had a rally planned Monday night to give a last boost to people who were going to take others to the polls and those who would be calling to get people out to vote. Then

Deb would have a victory rally on Tuesday. But this weekend was the purest form of politics. It was one person talking to another person, trying to convey the message and encourage them to vote. Then on to the next one.

I was buzzing all over town, keeping people happy and active. The response was generally positive. People get pounded by television and online ads for the big races, but there was almost no coverage of the races at the bottom of the heap. So people, once they get over their initial surprise and resistance to a stranger actually standing at their door, were generally pretty pleased that anyone was taking the time to ask them to consider voting for someone they probably hadn't heard of. This was, after all, the Midwest, where people are generally polite, at least on the surface. Even those who weren't planning to vote at all or were going to vote for Judge Hawthorne were not mean or rude.

It was early afternoon, and everything was running like clockwork. I was the model of efficiency — delivering flyers, yard signs, and drinks, ferrying people from one area to another and showing up where I was needed. I was doing a shopping run for cold drinks when Roger called me. He was not his usual talkative self. "Where's Deb?"

"She's doing the neighborhoods south of the mall between High and Rogers. Seems to be going well. No one has slammed doors. The volunteers are still at it."

"Do you know exactly where she is?"

"I can call her or Petunia. They're together. Is something wrong?"

"Hmmm . . .. Maybe . . .. Well, definitely something is wrong for someone, we just haven't decided if it's bad for Deb or not."

"What happened? "Where are you now?"

"I'm at the Marsh buying drinks and getting ice. I'm just about done. Want to meet me here?" "No. We need to get to Deb."

"I'm supposed to meet her at *The Inkwell* in fifteen minutes. She's going to take a break and get coffee for some of the volunteers."

"I'll meet you there." He hung up without giving me a chance to ask any questions. *Drama queen*, I thought as I paid and headed out to my car. I arrived at the town square and my inner goodness was rewarded with a parking spot nearly in front of the door. I stepped inside and the delightful smells of pastries, good food, and espresso drinks surrounded me. Deb was not in her usual place in the window but was at a table near the back. I suspect Petunia, who was sitting beside her, had insisted on a more secure location. I headed to their table. Deb pushed a mocha at me. She knew how to keep me happy. Slasher was at her feet, scarfing down a plate of yummies Tracy, the owner, had fixed for him.

"Roger called. What's blown up his skirt?"

I shook my head. "No idea. He told me to meet him here and hung up before I could ask."

Petunia had been watching the door. "Here he comes."

Roger hurried up to the table. Roger very rarely hurried. His usual walk was the definition of saunter.

Something was definitely up.

"Guess who's dead?" he said, sitting down. "Alexander the Great?" I suggested. "It can't be rock n' roll, because I've heard it will never die." "Who?" Deb asked. "What's happened?" "BurntHam," Roger replied. "That's why we haven't been able to find him. I thought he had slipped away and was up to something. Turns out, he slipped right off the mortal coil. They found him at the site of his development. Shot."

"Who do they think shot him?" I asked.

"Looks like suicide. He went out there yesterday and had a nice little picnic looking out over the lake. Drank most of a bottle of wine. Then *bam*, shot himself in the head. Some hikers found him this morning."

Deb looked at him. "How do you know about it? I doubt it's been on the news. Someone would have told me."

"I have friends on the force. They called." "You got any idea why?" Petunia asked.

"The note said it was money," Roger said. "Evidently, he was expecting money to bridge the gap before work started. It fell through and he was ruined."

"That means he didn't see a way out," Deb said. "So, that means he didn't think I would be pulling out before the election."

"So that means he wasn't the one hiring the bad guys," I said.

"Gee, BB. You have such a firm grasp on the obvious," Roger said.

"That means we concentrate on the judge," Petunia said. "What's the plan?"

"Nacho has a couple of Twinks prepping," Roger said. "The judge is going to have some door to door solicitation by some very willing and able young men.

I figure one of them will be able to entice the old fart into opening up in one way or another."

"You know I'd rather march over and confront the schmuck," Deb muttered.

“Won't accomplish anything," Roger said. "He'll deny it and you can't prove anything. He's mean, not stupid, except when he's thinking with his downstairs head. You'll just let him know he's getting to you. If anything, he'll turn up the pressure. He's going to anyway. He's got to get you to drop out by Monday at the latest. You can't drop out on Tuesday—that’s the election and once voting has started, he's lost."

"We should lay low until then," I said, thinking about sprays of bullets from passing cars.

Deb just stared at me. I remember that stare from my first-grade teacher, Mrs. White. She was a little lady, but when she whipped out *the stare*, the entire class went still. My sister is a teacher and when she was doing her student teaching, I happened to be visiting. At some point I made an untoward remark. From across the room, she whipped out *the stare*. It floored me. My little sister had somehow learned *the stare*. I wonder if there's a class in it. Deb hadn't been a teacher, but she had *the stare* down pat. I was immediately back in first grade and in trouble. I shut up.

Deb looked at Roger. "You understand that I will not be cutting back my campaigning, right? This is the crucial run up to the election. Today until dark and all day tomorrow we knock on doors. Monday is a string of interviews and that evening is the big rally to goose the volunteers to get out the vote. Everything has been building up to this."

Roger nodded and considered. "We can put more of Nacho's Twinks on door to door duty. We'll hit three houses at once. You and Petunia go to the house in the middle. Your volunteers along with a

Twink who is watching you will go to the house on either side. BB will be at the curb of the house where you are so he can get you out of there if necessary. Me or one of my people will be across the street watching. Then, you move on to the next three houses."

I studied Roger. My friend of many years, who had never given me a hint of this side of himself, was like a general planning a campaign. "You have people you can use for protection? More than Petunia? How could you keep this from me for so long?" I asked.

Roger smiled, reached across the table, and patted my head. "Don't blow a gasket, BB. After all this is over, we'll have a long talk. I didn't tell you about it because it would have made you too curious. Plus, you *know* you are not the world's best at keeping secrets."

"I can be discrete. I've never told anyone that Nacho was a field commander for *TaDah!*," I protested.

Roger shook his head. "You just did, sweet cheeks."

I felt a blush rise through my face. Roger pinched my cheek.

"No worries. Petunia and I have known about the Twinkie Army Destroying All Hypocrites for a while. And while Deb doesn't officially know, I'm sure she suspects. Nacho will be filling her in if she wins."

Deb started to speak, but Roger raised his hand to stop her. "If you are still alive."

"What about Monday night?" Petunia asked. "That's going to be a big crowd at the convention center with all the candidates and it's run by the Dems, not us. It's a hard place to secure. We can't do another bait and switch with TiaRa, the organizers won't allow it. Besides, it won't fool anyone again. No element of surprise."

"We'll put all our effort into getting the judge to confess before then. If we get to him and he calls off his dogs, then everything is groovy. The local police will be there Monday night and they'll be more than adequate if the judge folds. If not, we'll put everyone we have in the crowd and say our prayers."

"I can't imagine the judge would go this far just to hold on to power," Deb said.

"I can shed a little light there," Roger said. "I've been looking into BurntHam's finances, as well as the judge's."

"How?" Deb asked.

"Ask me no questions and I'll tell you no lies," Roger answered simply.

"But ...." Deb said.

Roger shook his head. "Trust me, you do *not* want to know. I have a lot of friends with interesting skill sets. I found some very questionable cash transactions. Several large sums, very large sums, were withdrawn from BurntHam's accounts. His private records," again he looked at Deb, "and save yourself the trouble of asking how I got a peek at his private records. His private records note them as 'Permit Process'. There were several line items. One had the notation 'F.H'. Now, the judge's name, if you recall, is Franklin Hawthorne and anyone who has taken even the quickest look at his lifestyle has noticed that the judge lives quite far above the means of someone living on a government salary."

"You think BurntHam was paying him bribes?" I asked.

"Again, that lightning-fast grasp on the obvious," Roger said. "And if that is the type of judge dear Hackie Hawthorne is, with all the building and lawsuits for zoning and developers putting up student housing without paying for infrastructure, there are potentially millions in bribes floating around to make sure that rulings go the right way. I've checked with Foxy and he doesn't have proof, but he has heard rumors." Roger looked at Deb. "That's why Hawthorne would go this far. He doesn't want to stop the flow of thank you cash. Plus, if he loses, there is a good chance some past contributions to his *buy my ruling fund* will come to light. That would mean prison and a chance to get up close and personal with some of the people he sent there."

Deb shook her head. "Well, that makes me all the more certain we've got to win this thing." She looked at me. "Come on, BB. Back to the sidewalks. I want to cover the entire southeast side tonight. Then we'll hit the northeast tomorrow." She slapped the table and stood. "Let's go."

"Petunia, you go with Deb," Roger said. "I'll go get our reinforcements in place. Deb, I want you to stay at Nacho's safe house tonight. No going home until this is over."

"What should I do?" I asked.

"Stay with her in your car at the curb," Roger said. "If you see anyone suspicious, throw yourself at them. The weight will incapacitate them."

"You can keep Slasher in the car," Deb offered. "I don't mind the risk, but I won't put him in danger. I'll leave him home tomorrow."

"That's a good idea," Roger said, "but I want you to have BB take him to your house. BB, I want you to stay out there tonight."

Deb began to protest, but Roger held up his hand. "I know you love that little pup, but I don't want you to risk taking him out in the middle of the night to pee. You might give away your position. They may know some of Nacho's safe houses and I don't want you to confirm where you are. Besides, he'll be happier at home."

"What about me?" I asked. "You don't want her at her house because it's dangerous, right?"

"Don't worry. If they break in, they'll see it isn't Deb. She's cuter. If they lob something at the house, it probably won't do any damage. I'll have someone swing by to check on you a couple of times. Plus, you'll be doing Deb a great service. You'll be a decoy."

"A decoy!"

"Yes. But look at the bright side. You'll have Slasher to protect you."

I looked hopelessly at the three of them. No joy.

Slasher and I were going to be spending the night together, and I was going to be a sacrificial goat.

I sighed and nodded. Dog watcher, briefcase handler, and now potential collateral damage. Again, I pictured the Christian Louboutin beaded loafers that awaited me at the end of this adventure. What must a girl do to get an absolutely lovely pair of shoes?

Chapter Twenty
Sunday

For once, the goat lived. No one attempted to kill me or burn down the house or perform any other unnatural acts during the night. Slasher woke me up a couple of times to remind me that his bladder was smaller than mine and allowed me to give him treats for accomplishing a pretty automatic task. Deb woke me far too early, mostly because she missed Slasher. She cooed at him excessively over the phone, but finally said goodbye. To thank me for my role as decoy and puppy pooper, she offered to pay for breakfast. As per instructions, and despite many doggie protests and casting of the hairy eyeball, I left Slasher ensconced on his favorite pillow, with a new pig's ear to chew on, and headed out to *The Inkwell*. On the way, I got a call from Roger.

"Ah, I guess you're not dead," he said.

"Yes, thank you very much. I didn't hear you swing by last night. Is that because you were quiet as a mouse or because you left me to my fate and went to bed?"

"I'll never tell. It would ruin the mystery."

"I'm off to *The Inkwell* to meet Deb. Want to join us?"

"Sorry, snookums. I have some judge investigating to do. He's been remarkably elusive, and I don't like that. With Petunia and Nacho's Twinks mixed in with the volunteers, Deb should be all right. You keep close to her and keep your eyes open. There's an off chance you might actually see or do something useful."

He hung up before I could respond with a snarky enough retort. By that time, I was at *The Inkwell*. I waved at Deb and ordered. Since she was paying, I made a point to aim for the expensive end of the offerings—a double mocha and two desserts. I figured I deserved it and I would walk off the extra dessert with all the canvassing ahead of us. Yes, I know I was slated to be in the car most of the time, but it was a good enough excuse when those pastries were giving me a come-hither stare.

I brought my sustenance to the table. "Where's the briefcase?" Deb asked. "I have precinct maps in it."

For once, I had forgotten the damn thing. I could picture it sitting on the kitchen table, where I had put it to make sure it wasn't left behind. Deb read the look on my face. "Never mind. You babysat Slasher. That's more important. I have a street map and that will be enough to plan the schedule. You can swing by later and get it. I *will* need the voter lists this afternoon."

"Sorry," I said. "But I am glad to know that you haven't had me hauling that thing around just to build upper body strength."

I ignored her condescending look and got down to the eating at hand. I am, after all, a growing boy. While I ate, Deb studied the street map and made notes and lists. As I finished, she handed me a schedule with people, streets to be covered, and times to check in. Deb was nothing if not well-organized. We were meeting the volunteers at her office, so off we went to rally the hardy souls.

After making copies and giving assignments and flyers to all those who had shown up, we headed out. It was one of those wonderful late fall days with a sparkling, deep blue sky. Many of the houses still had decorations and wilting jack-o-lanterns left from Friday's trick or treaters. Families were out taking down plastic witches and goblins and pulling fake spiderwebs from trees and bushes. I took a deep breath of the crisp air. I am not much of an outdoorsy guy, but even I appreciate days like this. It seemed inconceivable that anything bad could happen on such a day.

I try to avoid activities that involve conception, but inconceivable or not, we were about to be royally screwed.

I kept track of volunteers and made sure all were kept supplied with flyers, checklists, munchies, and drinks. I ran errands, kept communications going, and did whatever anyone asked me to do. Unfortunately, none of the Twinks that Nacho had assigned to keep watch over Deb asked me to do anything I spent quite a bit of time fantasizing about. Men. Those boys were interested in one thing and one thing only. Unfortunately, in this case, that one thing was Deb. Ah well, the fast pace did help the time whip by. Soon it was noon, and we headed back to the office where Deb had a nice spread for everyone. Lots of thank yous and lots of free food— that's what campaigns run on.

I was just sitting down to a lovely plate of bar-b-que and still-warm cornbread when Deb hurried up. "BB, I need you to run out and check on Slasher."

I nodded and took a bite. "Just as soon as I'm finished."

She put a hand on my fork. I looked up at her. Concern was writ large across her face. "I need you to go now. Look." She held out a greeting card. It had a picture of a chihuahua with a very sad expression, waving a paw. I opened the card. Printed in block letters were the words, 'Oh where, oh where has my little dog gone?'. "It was sitting in the middle of my desk. I called Roger right away." She took a deep breath, willing herself to keep it together. "He said I should stay here in case it's a trap. He said you have to go to my house and he'll met you there."

She grabbed my arm, her eyes glistening, holding back tears only by a huge effort of will. "Hurry, BB. Please. Go get Slasher."

I stood and gave her a quick hug. "On my way."

"Keep the card. Roger wants to look at it. No envelope." Her voice cracked. "Call me as soon as you get there."

I headed out at a jog. I exceeded speed laws and managed to get around the valium-besotted drivers meandering down the street. I got to Deb's house in record time. I jumped out of my car as Roger pulled up. We both headed toward the house, then stopped. The front door had been broken in. Nothing gentle or subtle. Splintered wood attested to a powerful force.

"Battering ram," Roger murmured. "Can't kick in a door that strong."

I let him go in first. He was, after all, the professional. I hung back just so I wouldn't get in his way.

"It's safe. No one here," he called out to me.

The room looked undisturbed. Nothing was out of place, no graffiti. Also, no little dog on a little pillow on the sofa wagging his tail in greeting. I tried calling out to him. Nothing. Now Slasher was not a shy dog. It was the height of restraint for him not to run up to anyone who came in, expecting a treat, a pat, and a lap. If I called and he didn't come, he wasn't there. However, to be sure, we made a quick pass through the house. While we were looking, Deb called Roger. He put her on speaker.

"Well?" she demanded.

Roger didn't mince words. "Not here." "What are we going to do?"

At this point, I was scanning the kitchen to see if Slasher's food bowl was there. It was. However, the briefcase that I had left in the middle of the kitchen table was not. In its place was a large envelope. I waved my arms to get Roger's attention and explained what had happened. He carefully opened the envelope and pulled out a single sheet of paper. In block letters it read, 'Nacho Mama's Patio Cafe. 2:30'.

Roger reported this to Deb.

"It's that damn Judge Hawthorne," Deb growled. "He's behind this." She had gone from a growl to a shout. "I'm going to his house right now and break him in half."

"He isn't there," Roger said.

"What? What do you mean?"

"I got a call from Petunia on the way over here. "Hawthorne's pet sheriff had a meeting with him this morning, but the judge wouldn't answer the door. The sheriff jimmied the lock. Hawthorne was lying in a puddle of his own filth, slipping in and out of consciousness. Alcohol poisoning. He must have been drinking since Friday afternoon. They took him to the hospital and he's out of danger, but he's not going anywhere."

"Then that's where I'm going," Deb stated. "Do you think that's a good idea?" I asked.

"We're talking about Slasher here, BB. He didn't take my dog himself. That's not how he operates. Wouldn't want to get his hands dirty. But he knows who did and he's going to tell me. You can come or not. I'm going to the hospital and get some damn answers." She hung up.

Roger looked at me. "We better get there quick. Deb has a slow fuse, but when she's about to blow, people are bound to get hurt. We may not be able to stop the avalanche, BB, but we might be able to keep her from killing the guy in front of witnesses."

I agreed. We both got in our cars and headed to the hospital. Roger called ahead to find out where the judge had been stashed. We got there in time to hear bellowing from the judge's room. Staff were running toward the noise. Deb must have just arrived, and mama was not channeling sweetness and light.

"You shit! You tired old misanthrope. What have you done with Slasher? Who took him? I will make you feel pain like you never imagined. Where is he? Tell me! I want my dog and I'm going to—"

We burst through the door a few steps in front of a cadre of nurses. Deb had grabbed the judge by the front of his hospital gown, along with a good handful of skin, and was dragging him up, shaking him like a crazed chocoholic attempting to get that last raisinette out of the box. The judge was flopping around like a rag doll. I'm not sure if he was conscious. The only thing coming out of his mouth was drool. Roger grabbed one side of Deb and I grabbed the other. We managed to tug her arms away from the judge, who fell back onto the bed. Nurses rushed up to him and began checking for damage. I turned around so I could whisper into Deb's ear, and also to prevent any searing of the eyeballs should an unplanned wardrobe malfunction result in public airing of the judge's privates.

"We've got to get out of here, Deb," I said. "Security is certain to be on the way and getting arrested for battery is not the way to win an election." She stood firm. "Not until he tells me who took Slasher and how I can get my dog back."

Roger began to argue, but suddenly, the judge whispered, "Dog? Doggie? I remember doggie. Patches. My doggie. Good boy. Come here, doggie. Give me kisses." Judge Hawthorne's light was on, but it was obvious that no one was home.

A nurse patted his hand. "Mr. Hawthorne, do you feel all right? Do you want some water? Does anything hurt?"

The judge looked at all of us gathered around his bed. I had an unbidden flashback of Dorothy waking up in Kansas, back from Oz. Did that make me Uncle Henry or Auntie Em? Perhaps one of the gay farmhands. The judge struggled to sit up, shaking me from my musings. He recognized Deb. A visitation of lucidity.

"Counselor," he said weakly, "good of you to come see me. It's over. I know that now. You win. You will make a fine judge." He drew a ragged breath. "I was just thinking about my old dog. He was my friend." We were losing him. Judge Hawthorne was fading away to memory lane. "I loved that dog. Do you have a dog? I love doggie doggie dog dog."

His eyes closed and he was out.

Roger looked at Deb. "It's not him. That is not someone who is planning to force you out of the race. Let's get out of here."

Deb nodded and allowed us to lead her out of the room. We quickly headed toward the elevators. The doors opened and several security guards stepped out. We let them pass and stepped in. The doors closed and down we went.

Deb sighed. "What now?"

Roger showed her the note. "Now we go to Nacho's and wait. It won't be long."

Chapter Twenty One
The Wait

When one of Nacho's Twinkie Army foot soldiers got too old to seduce and entrap hypocritical politicians and power brokers, they either sailed off into their own sunset or moved into management. The Twinks who had been keeping an eye on Deb during the door to door canvas were regular operatives who usually did less talking and less walking, wearing much less clothing. However, with Petunia, Roger, and I indisposed with the task of getting Slasher back unharmed, while keeping Deb from slipping into sorrow or kill mode, and the election looming, someone had to keep the volunteers coordinated, knocking, and talking. Nacho pulled in Josh, who was transitioning into leadership. He might have been getting too old for perv seduction duty, but he was stunningly age-appropriate for me. I had briefed him on the tasks and schedule, and I had tried hard to be professional. I was proud I managed not to lick his face. It was probably because I was on overload from too much stress over too short a time. Now he was off directing the volunteers—lucky devils — and I was sipping a drink at Nacho's while Deb paced and cursed. All our phones were out on the table, as we didn't know who would contact us or how. All we knew was that short note—'Nacho Mama's Patio Café. 2:30.'

Nacho was back in the office, probably arranging for Twinks to leap into action when the call came. I had no idea how large *TaDah*! was. I got the feeling that very few people knew. Lucky for us, Nacho was one of the few.

"It's after two-thirty," Deb growled. "Why haven't

we heard anything? If anything happens to that little dog, I'll ... " She stopped pacing and suddenly looked so sad.

Petunia, the immovable mountain, stood and grabbed Deb's shoulder. "Strength lady. Strength," she said. Then she pulled Deb into a hug. Stunning. I had never seen the smallest hint of emotion or tenderness from Petunia. I don't suggest she was mean. She was simply not built that way. Gravity or a planet simply exists. Those who ascribe emotions to such things are projecting. But now, the mountain hugged Deb and gave her comfort.

This amazing tableau was broken by one of Nacho's Twinks, who had been keeping watch out front, coming through the doors to the patio. Nacho barreled out of the office. "What's up?"

"I think it was a guy, but he had a helmet on," the boy said. "Zipped past the bar once on a little scooter, then circled back. Pulled out a hammer and shattered the window of a car right in front and tossed this in." He held out the missing briefcase.

Nacho nodded and took the case. "Thanks, Evan. You done good. Anybody follow the creep?"

Evan shook his head. "Billy tried, but the guy got away. Went down the bike lane, then disappeared. Billy's still circling around, trying to spot him, but I don't think he will."

Nacho shrugged. "Too bad, but probably wouldn'ta got much outta him anyway. You got the rest of the day off. Go have some fun. It's a college town. Might find some frisky student you can usher into manhood."

Evan winked and saluted. "Aye, aye, Cap'n." He went out. I watched him go, just to make sure his butt got out the door okay. I looked up and saw Roger leering at me. He knew me too well.

Nacho laid the briefcase on the table and nodded to Roger. "You got more experience with preserving evidence." Another unknown skill that Roger had kept from me. We were going to have quite a little talk once all this was over.

Roger nodded to Petunia, who pulled a pair of

thin latex gloves out of a pocket and carefully examined the case without opening it. She looked at Roger. “Doesn't look like it's wired."

"Okay. Open it up."

Petunia popped open the clasps and opened the case. Then she swiveled it around so we could all see. The law book and papers that had been in the case were still there, evidently untouched. However, in the middle, laying on top of them, was Slasher's collar and dog tag. At the bottom was a burner phone, with an envelope taped to it. Petunia pulled out a knife with a thin, sharp blade and slit it open. She pulled out a piece of paper and opened it on the table. It read:

> "Record a video statement that you are officially withdrawing from the race and cannot serve because of a serious medical condition.
> Write a statement in your own handwriting that says the same thing.
> Sign it. Make a video of you signing it. Put a copy of the videos on a thumb drive.
> Put the thumb drive and signed statement in an envelope.
>
> Tomorrow at noon, you will receive a call on this phone giving you instructions where to drop the package.
> You will not try to trace the call. You will follow instructions exactly.
> Do not bring the phone with you. Do not bring any phone or device which allows anyone else to track you.
>
> Once you drop the package, go to your house.
> Once we get the package, we will copy and distribute the materials to election officials and news outlets.
> We will then disappear.
>
> If you follow these instructions, you will be told

where to find your dog unharmed.
If you do not follow these instructions exactly, your dog's body will turn up . . . someday.
We have no wish to hurt your dog. Do what we want, and all will turn out right.
Make a fuss or bring in any of your faggot friends or the police to help, and your little puppy will suffer because of you."

I looked at Deb. Have you seen high speed photography of a water balloon that has been stuck by a pin? The form of the balloon is still there, in part held by the water and in part by the retreating skin of the balloon. The form is there, but the collapse is inevitable. It's just a matter of time. Deb swayed on her feet. Roger grabbed a chair with one hand and guided her to sit with the other. Deb was one of those people you hoped to have around in a crisis, yet she was crumbling. I think that over the years we develop a thick skin to get through the slings and arrows that life seems to delight in pitching our way. However, to preserve any glimmer of humanity, we absolutely must maintain a few soft spots where our heart can be touched. If we pave over every spot, we cannot be hurt, but we cannot feel or truly be alive. This is why art is essential to life. It feeds our deepest need to be more than a bag of water that consumes and excretes. Slasher was one of those spots for Deb and someone had plunged an arrow right in the middle of it.

She drew a long, tortured breath, looking down and far away. Then, having decided, she looked up at us. "I quit," she said softly. "I wouldn't be alive without Slasher. There has to be a difference between the mission and the woman. I cannot, will not, give up this part of me so I can win a position. Everyone has a lever. Everyone has something that they hold too dear to give up. Slasher is my soft spot and they found it. I'll do what they want."

Nacho put a hand on Deb's shoulder. "You can't do that, sweetheart. You can't."

Deb looked up at Nacho, no energy to fight, but no intention of changing her mind.

"You can't give in," Nacho said. "It ain't about you

and your position or even this election. Hell, judge or not, in fifty years, no one will know the difference. It's about whether you stand alone to face the world or are part of something. I don't mean *the movement*. Only movement I care about is done in the privacy of my bathroom. I mean how you feel you fit into the world. If you think it's you alone against everybody and everything, then you got a lonely road ahead." Nacho gestured to the rest of the table with that disgusting, cheap cigar that always smoldered, divine incense from the ass of the gods. "You got us, and you got to trust that we can find this crap head and get your baby back. When it comes down to it, who you gonna rely on to steer you right—us or some unknown dog thief?"

Deb considered. Nacho's words seemed to pump her up. I could see her mind spark, turn over, sputter a few times, then kick in. She looked around. "Okay.

Here's the deal. I am going to record the statement, sign the paper, and transfer it to a thumb drive."

"But—" I began.

Deb held up her hand. "I'm not finished. However, I will rely on all of you to catch whoever is responsible before they can turn it over to the media." Her eyes flashed and I saw unbridled malevolence in her face. "Then, turn that scum over to me and I will take care of them."

Nacho slapped her on the back. "Done. Now get out of here and let Roger and me work our magic. Leave the note. I want to examine it more closely. Petunia, you go with her, just in case there are some other surprises planned."

"What should I do?" I asked.

Nacho snorted. "Anything you want as long as it's somewhere else."

Deb said, "Come with us, BB. I want to go to the office. I've got a couple of interviews tomorrow and if I'm still in the race, I want to be prepared. Plus, we have the volunteers coming for dinner and I have to be there or everybody will know something is wrong. Besides, if I don't keep busy, I'll go nuts." She stood and headed out. Petunia and I followed.

Nacho called out, "Back here at ten in the morning. We need to be ready before noon."

"I'll have the thumb drive with the recording and the statement," Deb said.

"Make a couple of copies of both," Roger suggested. "Who knows, they might come in handy. And why not bring a blank thumb drive and an envelope with a blank piece of paper, just for shits and giggles."

Deb considered, then nodded.

Chapter Twenty Two
Monday Morning

Ten o'clock is a reasonable time to start the day. It was a little slice of heaven not joining the dawn patrol that Deb and Slasher had demanded. I was awake, aware, and ready to face whatever got thrown my way when we all met again at *Nacho Mama's*. *Hoosier Daddy* was still closed as any but the seediest of bars should be that early on a Monday, but Roger opened the door soon after I texted my arrival. Everyone else was already there. Nacho and Roger looked a bit worse for the wear. I suspected that neither had slept. Nacho had pulled a coffee maker out to the table and had serious caffeine for all. I usually prefer milk and sugar in mine, but some days, just like some nights, black and bitter was the way to get the job done.

Roger and Nacho had worked out a detailed plan involving alternating teams of Twinks on different modes of transportation set to follow Deb once the call came. Deb had three envelopes, each containing a sheet of paper and a thumb drive. One was the original. One was a copy. The third had blanks. Everyone was discussing different contingencies and time was rolling by. Soon the dreaded phone call would come. I had nothing to offer and knew that if I tried making something up to seem clever or important, I would be on the receiving end of a biting comment. Instead, I drank my coffee and tried to look thoughtful. The letter from yesterday was laying on the table. Roger had said it held no fingerprints and no significant clues. I picked it up and looked at it, hoping for some deep insight. There was a bit of a blotch near the edge of the paper. I brought it close to get a better look. I caught a faint whiff of something. I held the blotch up to my nose and sniffed.

"BB, if you need to blow your nose, do not use that," Roger said, breaking off from his conversation with Nacho.

Everybody looked at me and I felt a bit embarrassed.

"I thought I smelled something," I said.

"I think that every time you come near," Roger said.

This was too much. I knew I was of no use when it came to strategizing attacks on bad guys, but there was something familiar about that smell. I took another big sniff. Then it struck me.

I was back in Judge Walker's drawing room with that snotty assistant giving me the evil eye while Deb was in the garden, not quite getting endorsed by all the high and mighty society muffs at the *Ladies' Garden Club and Debate Society*. I had seen the bottle of lotion on the desk and had committed the grave offense — according to Leticia — of trying to take a squirt of it to help calm my nerves after nearly being blown up. I remember her exact words, "The judge has it made especially for her in France. It is her own personal scent, and no one is to use it but her."

I looked up from my little flashback into the slightly amused, partially annoyed faces of Nacho, Roger, Deb, and Petunia. "The judge," I said.

Roger shook his head. "Early onset dementia, BB? Remember, we saw him yesterday. No way he could be behind this."

"Not that judge. Judge Walker." I explained.

Nacho poked me in the chest. "Are you sure, BB? Very, very sure? Sure enough that you are willing to risk how much I will hurt you if you are wrong?"

"Then it will be my turn," Roger added. "And of course, Petunia will want a shot."

It was intimidating, these three looming over me, but I know my hand lotions. I sniffed. "I know what I smell on this page and I know what I smelled then. I had never smelled it before. It wasn't exactly to my taste. A bit too heavy on the lavender, but a nice ping of sage after and...."

I knew I was babbling, but those three were making me nervous. I am aware of my limitations, but I am also aware of my strengths, and hand cream, well, I may not be a professional, but I can be classed as a very knowledgeable amateur. I started to explain this when Roger reached over and closed my mouth, holding it closed for a moment.

"Enough, dear. I will stipulate to your knowledge of hand cream, for *whatever* purpose." He turned to the others. "We've got to surprise her. There's a good chance she'll have the dog there and send her lackey out to collect the booty."

"Wait a minute," Deb said. "You are talking about swooping down on a respected judge. A judge who has not quite, but almost endorsed me. Why would she go to such extremes to get me to withdraw? What would she gain?"

Nacho had a good handle on what evil lurks in the minds of men and women. "Same reason as Judge Hawthorne. Roger, you said there were a bunch of odd chunks of cash going out of BurntHam's funds that you figured for bribes, right?"

Roger nodded.

"BurntHam wouldn't risk it all on Hawthorne. That guy is too squirrely. BurntHam would have covered all his bases. Walker must be taking incentives, just like Hawthorne. If Deb gets in, there's no way that doesn't come to light. She needs everything to stay the same, but can't openly support Hawthorne, so she's got to get rid of you."

"But Hawthorne is out of the picture," Deb said.

"Nobody but us knows that," Roger countered. "Petunia got the tip about him from a friend at the hospital. He's there under an alias. No word has gotten out. He's got plenty of pull."

Deb nodded. "Okay. It makes sense. What do we do?"

Nacho and Roger both pulled out their phones and started calling, barking orders. After a few minutes, Nacho looked at Deb and me. “We're going to crash her little party. We've got groups moving into position now. Foxy’s going to meet us there and use his charm and pull to get inside. Then we’ll swoop in. Deb, you go to your office and be seen by as many people as you can. I want it to be absolutely clear that you did *not* have anything to do with what is about to happen. The boys are bringing around a couple of cars. Roger and Petunia, let's go have some fun."

"What about me?" I asked.

Nacho grinned. "Stay here and finish your coffee, sweetheart. Then have another. Keep an eye on all the stuff here. That is, unless you want to take part in a raid. Might be just the butch you need to make you a man."

I shook my head. “I'm very happy to stay here, thank you very much. It's safer."

“That's what I thought, cream puff." Nacho looked around at the others. "Okay, let's head out. It's time to end this thing."

They were gone in a flurry, and I was left with a half a pot of coffee and a bit of quiet me time. I gave a contented sigh. The melodrama was ending. I wondered how inopportune it would be to slip inside the bar and add a bit of Kahlua and maybe a spot of brandy to my coffee, just to make it a little more palatable. After another swallow of the bitter sludge, I decided that passing up the opportunity of a full bar would be nearly criminal, so I slipped inside *Daddy's* and embellished my drink. Then I went back out to the patio and happily enjoyed the morning calm. It was a lovely feeling to be alone inside a bar, like I'd been allowed backstage at a theater before the actors showed up. I was privy to an event just itching to happen. I was mingling with the runners just before the beginning of a race. Of course, at *Daddy's* any races weren’t a sprint, but a slow, rolling jog to an unknown destination. Fun to sip my coffee and consider the races I had run on this particular track.

My reverie was broken by a call. It was Roger.

"You fucked the pooch, BB," he said grimly. "We showed up just as she was pulling up. She was returning from a weekend out of town. Thankfully, Foxy talked to her first, not Nacho. Foxy has charm and subtlety and Nacho is . . . how shall I say, more direct. She was offended. Very offended."

"But couldn't that just be a cover?"

"You weren't here. No one is that good an actor. She drew herself up and could have frozen ice with her glare and we hadn't come close to accusing her. It took all the charm Foxy had to get her to talk to us and tell us where she'd been."

"And?" I asked.

"She has been at a judicial conference in St. Louis for the last three days, so she had plenty of very respectable witnesses. In addition, she *did* know about Judge Hawthorne, because he wasn't there and, evidently, judges like to gossip as much as anyone else."

"But what about the lotion?"

"I couldn't very well ask about that, could I? Not without accusing her. I'm sure it's not off the shelf, but I'm willing to bet they don't make it just for her, despite what her assistant said. I think she was just making a big deal about it because you dared to touch her precious judge's stuff. Someone else must have the same made-only-for-them lotion."

"Damn. How much trouble am I in?" I asked.

Roger sighed. "Well, you aren't going to get any kisses from Nacho any time soon. I don't think you'll be banned. You noticed something and we ran with it. I have to admit that it was a pretty good catch. Unfortunately, not all catches turn golden. Yours turned out to be a turd."

My face flushed. "I'm sorry. I'm really—"

"It's okay, BB. It didn't work out. It happens. Unfortunately, she called the cops to check us out. We'll be able to clear things up, but it will take a little while. Once we're finished, we'll head back there. Watch the stuff. I'll call Deb and once we're all back, we'll figure out what to do next."

He disconnected.

I stared at the table, covered with papers, cups, and the ever-present briefcase. Shit. I thought this particular unpleasant dance was over—we'd get Slasher back and the election would happen, and then I could buy my shoes and go back to fluffing exhibits for Dustyn. But no. No joy. No luck. No good. Lots of no and the looming horror of Deb withdrawing and the strong possibility that sweet Slasher was going to end up dead.

There are times it is hard to breathe because it just doesn't seem worth it. Whatever is coming with that next breath is not worth the effort to suck in air. I sat and stared and struggled to convince myself to inhale each time my lungs asked for some oxygen.

A phone rang. Confusing. Not my phone. My phone plays a fake calypso tune so I can anticipate a party every time it rings. This was an old-fashioned ring—how dull. Did someone leave their phone? Not likely. People were more apt to forget a foot than their phone. Phones are everyone's constant companions today. Used to be strange to see a table full of people ignoring each other and looking at their phones. Now phones are part of the conversation.

I looked at the table. Then I realized it was the burner phone that had come with the kidnapper's note. It was *the* phone. It was ringing, and I was the only one here to answer it and if I didn't, then Slasher was dead for sure, but if I did, I had no idea what to do. It rang again. If I didn't answer, they would hang up and the door to hope would slam shut. I looked at the double doors that led into *Hoosier Daddy*, willing someone to burst through and get the phone, but no.

Ring!

I couldn't do nothing. I grabbed the phone and hit talk.

"Y-yes?"

"Who the hell is this?" The voice was mechanical, obviously filtered through some kind of device. I couldn't tell anything about the caller, not even if they were a man or woman.

"I'm BB."

"Well, who the hell are you, BB? Where is the candidate?"

"She . . . er . . . she had to go to her office."

"She isn't there!? Doesn't she care about her dog at all? Who else is there?"

"No one. They all had to go to Deb's office."

"So they don't want to even try to save this little ankle biter? No one gives a shit about this poor little dog?"

"No . . . Yes. Stop. Please! Deb cares the world for Slasher. We all do." My eye fell on the envelope that held her statement and the thumb drive. "She left what you want with me. I can bring it to you. Or you can wait, and she'll be back in a few minutes."

"No. No waiting. Everything is planned to the minute. I'm not going to give her a chance to set up some kind of trap. It's all up to you. Do not call anyone. Do not leave a message. You have to do it and follow orders exactly, or you know what's going to happen, right? Can you follow orders?"

My heart was pounding. This was way too adventurous for me, but I didn't see any alternative. At least, not one that I could live with. I nodded. "I can follow orders."

"Good. Leave now. Right now. Come alone and leave no hint of where you are going. We are watching the front door of that fag club. If we see more than one person come out, it's over. You'll never hear from us again. Do you understand?"

I nodded.

"Do you understand?" the voice demanded again.

I realized I hadn't replied. "Yes. I'll do what you say."

"Leave immediately. Drive to Rose Hill Cemetery. It's only a few minutes away. You must know where it is."

"I do."

"Do you know where Hoagy Carmichael's grave is?"

"Sure. West end, near the doughnut shop."

"Go there and walk north. Just before the wall, you'll see a mausoleum. It's just a little one. There are family graves around the front of it. The mausoleum has a metal grill and glass door that's locked. You'll find a small bag hanging on the door with a bouquet of flowers. Take the flowers and put the envelope that contains what we asked for in the bag. Then put a flower on each of the graves out front. Keep your back to the door of the mausoleum. Do not miss a single grave. Do not look back at the mausoleum. We'll be watching. If you do not follow these directions exactly, the dog will die. Do you understand?"

"Yes."

"Can you follow orders?"

"Yes."

"Then do it. Now. Do not take your phone. Do not take this phone. We will be able to check. You have two minutes to leave. If we don't see you leave within the next two minutes, you might as well not come at all. Do you understand?"

"Yes." The phone disconnected. I looked around. I was on my own. I had to leave my phone. I hated that. One of the kidnappers was probably planning to break into the bar, steal it, and I'd never see it again. I left it on the table. I scooped up all the papers and put them in the briefcase. I put the envelope with the statement and thumb drive on top of everything. I considered taking out the heavy law book Deb kept in the damn thing but decided something that big was probably expensive and I didn't want to buy her a new one if whoever broke in decided to take or deface it. Then I snapped the case closed and headed out. I didn't dare leave a note. It was just me and my terror. On a nice day, when I wasn't involved in a dognapping, the cemetery was close enough to walk to. Today I headed to my car and drove. It only took a couple of minutes.

Rose Hill Cemetery is overgrown with peonies. Not a rose in sight. I guess Peony Hill was too open to slight mispronunciation, which might lead to euphemistic confusion that it is a rutting spot, not a resort for the dead. It was not grand or huge, but was a nice place to walk, look at faded tombstones, and contemplate days and lives gone before. No 'I am Ozymandius' faux temples, but several past powers within the university and town resided there. You could also visit wives who had given up their first and last names to be known forever as Mrs. Frank Whoever. Soldiers with death dates far too close to their birth date reminded any who cared of the glory

of war. And an infant's row with names and only the date of death huddled together in a corner. Hoagy Charmichael had written songs and sung them all the way to Hollywood and still came back. Long before I knew of Magawatta, I knew of Cricket, Bogie, and young and beautiful Lauren in *To Have and Have Not*, which was rewritten to be a rerun of Casablanca, but with Hoagy as Dooley and Lauren as Ingrid. Yes, Hoagy was a Magawatta son and to Magawatta he returned, whatever remained of him sitting near enough to the doughnut shop to wish the dead could rise. I parked nearby, checked again that I had put the proper envelope so that it was easy to reach in the briefcase, and headed up the hill.

There were always a few people around. It was a good place to walk a dog and the city provided poop bags at regular intervals, which surprisingly, were used. Some respect for the dead, I guess. I saw a small family group near one of the stones, laying plastic flowers to memorialize their deep feelings of loss. I never have been able to understand putting fake flowers on a grave. It seems to be sending the wrong message. As I headed up a hill, I passed a new grave, dirt piled high and no stone placed yet. Kneeling toward the front of the pile, a small form in a dark dress and heavy veil rocked back and forth, quietly weeping and babbling her misery. I walked by quietly, not wanting to impose on her grief. There was enough unhappiness and angst swirling around me. No need to share.

A bit farther up the hill, a circular walkway, barren of flowers in November, led to a mausoleum. It was small—about four telephone booths pushed together. It was plain, gray limestone. No ornamentation. No carving. Just the name East above the door. I've seen more ornate storage sheds. If it wasn't on the north side of the cemetery, I would have thought it was a city structure—one mausoleum for each direction, built with minimal expenditure. The only flourish was the door itself, which had a rather ornate bit of grill work and heavy, very scratched glass. A chain threaded through the grill work and a large padlock kept any but the most industrious thieves or visitors out. It seemed like overkill, as it were. Only the most optimistic or desperate thief would look at the plain décor and expect to find anything of value. Hanging from the chain, as the caller had said, was a bag that held a bouquet of cheap flowers. Someone had spared every expense. However, it was not for me to judge — at least, on the basis of flowers. I opened the briefcase and pulled out the envelope. I removed the bouquet and put the envelope in. Then I picked up the briefcase in one hand and the bouquet in the other and looked for the gravestones the dognapper had mentioned. They were not hard to find.

The mausoleum was apparently too small for the extensive East family, because all around it, on either side, were grave markers. There would be a largish stone with the name East carved into it. Clustered around these stones would be a group of markers that only had initials, not full names. I laid a flower on H.R. East. A. G. East and H. P. East. Then I noticed A. L. East. *A LEast*, I thought, with a smile. Then a A. B. East. I put two flowers there, hoping to sooth it if it was savage. I continued around behind the structure, laying flowers on stones. The East family had certainly gone forth and multiplied. "I wonder if there is a Yolanda in the family," I said to myself. "She'd be the one to resurrect, since she would certainly rise. There's A. F. They must be friends, because you need Yeast for a Feast."

My punning was interrupted by a muffled bark. I looked around. It was coming from the mausoleum.

Could Slasher be locked inside? I headed that way, planning to get that door open one way or another. Maybe I could break the glass with the briefcase. It was solid and my aching arm could attest to the fact that it was heavy.

However, as I arrived once again in front of the door, my way was blocked. The lady in black had risen from the grave down the hill, stopped keening, and walked up to the mausoleum. Her back was to me, but I could see she had taken the envelope from the bag and had pushed her veil up to be able to study the contents. As I ran up, she turned and I received two very unpleasant shocks. The first thing I noticed was that she held a gun in her hand. I am not a gun person. I don't know much about them and haven't held one since I shot a rifle in boy scouts oh so many years ago. However, just as cars seem designed to say 'I am fun and shiny and go fast', this was obviously designed to say, 'back the fuck up, because I can and will hurt you quickly and certainly and will be very glad to do it!'.

My eyes traveled from the gun up to the face of the woman. Twisted, not in the sorrow of loss, but in anger with a big dash of distaste, was Betina Leticia East, Judge Walker's pandering assistant.

"Get your hands up. Now!"

I raised my hands. The briefcase was heavy, and I moved to put it down. She waved the gun. "Stop! I said put your hands up. Keep them up."

"But I just want to put the — "

"Did I ask you what you wanted? Do I care what you want? No. Keep your damn hands up or I will shoot you right in your fat faggot middle."

Now that was just cruel. I'm used to being called a faggot—that washes over me. But fat? Unkind. I was about to point out that I had been dieting and exercising, maybe not as much as I could or even should, but I was trying, when little Miss I've-Got-a- Gun-and-a-Bad-Attitude decided she had more to say.

"What's the matter?" she spat out. "Was the high and mighty dyke too important to come rescue her puppy wuppy? She sent you," she sneered at me, "her two-legged dog. Go fetch, doggie."

Leticia was pacing back and forth, gesturing with her gun. "It's always up to us, the assistants, to get the important things done. They get the headlines, but we are the ones who do what is necessary, even if it isn't easy or pleasant." She waved the gun back and forth, like it was her finger. "It's up to us."

I stared at her. Every hair was still in place. Perhaps she used lacquer. There was no question that her mind had taken a pleasant little vacation from reality and what had been left behind was not happy or sane. She motioned to the envelope. "This will take care of your dyke. You understand why we could not allow her to win, don't you?"

I didn't really know what to say, but she obviously wanted an answer. I could only muster a shrug and looked confused. That part was easy, because I had no idea what was going on. "Did Judge Walker tell you to do it?" I asked. "I thought she was out of town. And while we're talking, do you mind if I put down this briefcase? It's really heavy."

"Keep it lifted, Nancy Boy. Maybe it will build up some muscles." Leticia gave a mirthless laugh. "My judge doesn't know anything about this. She shouldn't. She can't. She is above such mundane things."

Leticia looked off into the distance as if communing with God. "Judge Walker is a great lady and cannot be besmirched by everyday necessities. That is why I am so important to her. I understand what she needs, even before she does. One day, she will be on the Supreme Court of the United States."

Leticia glared at me, daring me to contradict her.

I used an old trick my mother taught me. Just repeat what they said, but phrase it as a question. This makes the listener know you are paying attention and feigns support. "The Supreme Court?" I asked.

"Yes, of course," she said. "Soon there will be an opening on the state supreme court, and Judge Walker's years of service and dedication make her appointment a certainty. After that, her knowledge and style will shine like a beacon and an appointment to the national court will be inevitable."

She turned to me, a gentle smile on her face as she contemplated the divine goodness that was her boss.

Then her face twisted into a mask of madness and rage as she considered me and my ilk. "Until you and your shameless hag stepped in the way of those better than any of you."

She held the gun as if it was a flaming sword of righteousness. "You would try to stop her, but I could not allow such obscenities to profane our march to glory. And now I have the means to stop your boss and all that remains is tying up loose ends."

She was completely lost in her madness. She just needed a Wagnarian score to back her up. Unfortunately, she stopped talking to an unknown audience and directed her attention and her gun back at me. "Together, my judge and I will go to Washington and take our place in history. She as the judge and me as her faithful assistant. And this is where the real journey begins." She gestured around to the graves. "Right here amidst my family, who never thought a girl would amount to anything. Especially me, for I am an East. I am Betina Leticia East. When I was a girl, they all called me Letty. I still remember them chanting, 'Letty East. Letty East. She's the Least East that Letty East." She glared at me.

"Everyone knew the East family only put initials on their graves, so they called me Least East. What they didn't know was that my name wasn't Letty, it was Betina. Lettie isn't even my middle name. My mother wanted me to be named Leticia after her mother. My father didn't like the name and didn't like Granny. He was the one who filled out the paperwork and he named me after his mother, Betina and didn't give me a middle name. My mother called me Letty and she never forgave my father because my full name is Betina East. I'm not the Least. I am the BEAST."

With that, she aimed the gun at me. It occurred to me that she was not just going to take the documents and destroy Deb's election. She was going to make sure no one knew who was behind it. She was going to shoot me. I was going to be a casualty of an insane person who had fallen in love with her boss and thought she was going to make her a Supreme Court judge. I was not going to get those Christian Laboutin beaded loafers. I was going to get a very unbecoming hole in some part of my body, and I was going to bleed all over some strangers' cemetery plots before someone stumbled across my corpse and had to undergo years of therapy to come to grips with what a cruel world it is.

And this was wrong, wrong, wrong. And when we are faced with something that is obviously wrong, we can hide our heads and wait for it to rip us apart or we can do something, no matter how impotent it might turn out to be. And I was not going to go quietly. At least not holding up this damn, heavy briefcase. So, I hurled it with all my insubstantial might right at Ms. Betina East, the Beast.

An edge of the case caught her full in the face, knocking her back and opening up a wound that was sure to leave a scar. With a shout of surprise, she fell back. The gun went off with an enormous boom. I fell to the ground, my ears ringing, my eyes squeezed shut, my arms wrapped around my head. If I wasn't dead yet, I was sure I was going to be soon. I know that what goes up invariably comes down and with my luck, I was going to be killed by a falling bullet. However, Saint Lance was looking out for me yet again. The bullet hit a statue of an angel nearby and fell among some gravestones. No worries. Everyone over there was already dead.

I lay still, unsure what to do next. Was this the end? Was she still there just lining up another shot? I was too scared to run. Then I heard shouts and running footsteps. Hands took hold of me, pulling my arms off my head and hoisting me to my feet. I looked around, frightened and confused. Roger. It was Roger. He grabbed me into a hug, then held me out at arm's length, exploring me for damage, then planted a big, wet kiss on my lips and pulled me into another hug.

"How did you—" I asked.

"Joshie. We had him stationed at the bar just in case anything happened. He saw you head out and called us. You don't think we trust you to be on your own, do you?"

I struggled back and looked around. Petunia was holding crazy Betina's arms behind her back in what looked like — and I hoped was — a very painful hold.

Blood was streaming down the BEast's face from where the briefcase had hit her. She must have a bit of the old SM in her, because her face seemed to be battling between religious fervor and erotic ecstasy.

A small cadre of police encircled the area. Detective Crawford stepped forward and took the BEast from Petunia, read her rights, and began to lead her away. At the edge of the group, crazy Betina pulled away from the policeman and turned back.

"Get that creature away from my family!" she shouted. No one moved. No one understood. "That damned little mutt. If it shits on my ancestors, I will destroy it. Get that disgusting thing out of there."

Deb snapped to what she was saying. She walked over to the crazy lady. "Slasher? Is Slasher in the mausoleum?"

"Of course, you idiot. Where else would it be? And if that little rat soils my — "

"The key," Deb shouted. "Where is the key?"

"Around my neck. Where else would it be? It's around my neck."

Deb looked at Detective Crawford for permission. He nodded. Around the madwoman's neck was a silver chain. Deb grabbed a handful of Betina's hair and twisted hard, holding her head immobile. With her other hand she grabbed the chain and yanked. It broke easily and from its dainty links hung a key. Deb shoved her face right into Betina's. "You can fuck with me, bitch, but don't ever fuck with my dog." Deb looked like she was going to take a bite out of Betina, but Petunia put a hand on her shoulder.

"Let her be. We're all okay and all she's got is her crazy to keep her company."

Deb looked at Petunia, took a long, difficult breath, let go of Betina's hair and turned away. As Crawford led the crazy lady off to jail, Deb hurried over to the mausoleum. The key easily turned in the lock and the chain came off, the door swung open, and Slasher bounded out. He leapt into Deb's arms, covering her face with kisses.

Chapter Twenty Three
And In The End

The rally that night went as smooth as a hot tub full of olive oil. Nacho's Twinks were there in case any stray hit men hadn't gotten the message that their contractor was on her way to a nice long stay in a rubber room where she and Napoleon could strategize and debate whether to take over Russia or the United States. Turns out the Twinks weren't needed. The only surprise was when Judge Walker showed up and gave a very long and very ringing endorsement of Deb. She privately apologized to Deb at great length.

"I shall spend the rest of my career attempting to make it up to you, Ms. Eubank," she said. "I had no idea and that is my crime. I should have been aware. I am ashamed. You should know that Leticia has confessed to everything. She mostly acted alone. She is very strong and resourceful. When she needed muscle, violence, or expertise she lacked, she used a list of contacts she had developed over the years using my case files. Some she offered money. Some she offered favors. She proudly turned over a list of all the people she had contacted over the years. The police have already visited each of them and explained where suspicion would fall should anything happen to you."

Deb grinned and pulled her into a hug. "Judge, we are going to have some fun together. Imagine a cloak room without the smell of Hawthorne's alcohol- based sweat."

The judge smiled. "You could smell that from the defense table?"

Deb nodded. "And if you got him after lunch, it

mixed with the mints he used to cover his liquid lunch."

Judge Walker shook her head. "You are correct. I will not miss that at all."

Roger stood close and had heard the conversation. "What about BurntHam?" he asked.

The judge stared at him a moment, deciding how to handle someone who not only had eavesdropped on a private conversation, but also had injected himself into it. Roger just grinned at her. He gave everyone equal billing. No blame until proven guilty. Respect where respect was due. After a moment, she smiled back at him.

"She was responsible for that, too. She was very proud of how she had manipulated him. She convinced him that she was taking bribes for me. That's where she got the money to hire her accomplices." A look of pure rage flashed across her face, but she quickly stilled it with a shake of her head and looked directly at Deb. "Let me be clear. I have never considered taking money or favors for my judgments. She could not have struck a more cruel blow. It is absolutely against everything I hold dear. I need you to know that."

This was not posturing. We all saw it.

"I understand," Deb said. "We live in the same place, Judge. We may disagree on interpretation, but when we do," Deb gave her a cocky grin, "I'll know it's just because you got it wrong."

The judge laughed. Actually laughed. "You are right, Ms. Eubank. This is going to be fun."

"But BurntHam. Did she shoot him?" Roger asked.

"Yes. She was happy to give the details. She had worked on seducing him. From what I heard, Mr. Burns was always interested in forbidden fruit. Being able to bed the assistant to a judge appealed to him.

She convinced him that she would give herself to him and arranged to meet him. She brought a picnic and drugged the wine. When he was compliant, she put a gun in his hand and helped him pull the trigger."

"An industrious little scamp, wasn't she?" Roger said.

The judge did not answer. She surveyed the room, full of volunteers ready to hit the phones and the streets the next day to get out the vote. "I have taken up enough of your time. I will leave you to it. Again, I am sorry for not ferreting out my assistant and causing you so much grief."

Deb cocked her head. "Psychos are hard. They believe they are touched by God, instead of just being touched."

The judge nodded. "I shall see you at your swearing in, if not before."

The next day was a blur of errands. The turnout was huge and shortly after the polls closed, Deb was declared the winner. The victory party was at *Hoosier Daddy*, with endless food and drinks provided by Foxy. Everyone was there and in a joyous mood. TiaRa put on a show but insisted on having Deb, robe bedecked, sitting on a throne on stage the entire evening. A steady stream of well-wishers came on stage to have their picture taken with the new judge- to-be. It was like a grownup visit to Santa.

I was given Slasher duty in a chair nearby. The damn briefcase had been taken into evidence, so would trouble my life no more. That was the cherry on top of the glorious sundae of freedom from the angst of the last ten days. I was glad that Deb had won, but I was overjoyed that the whole thing was over. I sat quietly stroking Slasher, looking across the crowd, happy for the absence of worry or fear of attack.

I was watching a little movie in my head. I was walking into a grand shoe store. The snotty little queen who was working there looked me up and down with undisguised disdain, obviously hoping I would realize this store was out of my league and price range and go to Shoes R Us. I sat down and when it became obvious that I wasn't going to leave, he twittered up to me dripping attitude in his wake. And then I asked for my shoes. My Christian Louboutin Aqualac Beaded Loafers. And the look on the face of that little poof wannabe morphed from disdain to enormous respect as he realized that he was standing in the presence of a true devotee of fashion and taste.

He was just about to take my foot and nestle it into his crotch before slipping those perfect loafers onto my feet when Roger sat down beside me and tapped me on top of my head.

"Wake up, BB. You're living in one of your fantasies. I can tell."

Coming slowly out of the splendid moment, I looked at him. "So what?" I grumped. "I deserve it. In case you haven't noticed, I've had a rough week."

Roger pinched my cheek. "Aww. Poor, BB. Didums have to work hawd? Wassums skeerd?"

I slapped his hand away. "Fuck off, Roger. You know I was out of my comfort zone. And you also know you got some 'splainin to do."

"That's what I want to talk to you about," he said. "You did all right this week. In your own way, you handled things. When it counted, you weren't nearly as incompetent as you let on."

"Wow. Thanks, mister. You say the nicest things."

He ruffled my hair. "Sure, son."

I slapped his hand away. "Quit."

"You deserve some answers," he continued. "I'll lay it all out for you when you have had a chance to recover, but for now, I have an offer."

"No, I will not bear your child."

"As if. But here's the deal. Yes, I do have a private, very private agency. There's a lot of things I do for a lot of clients. We focus exclusively on gay clients. That's why we're called the LnL Detective Agency."

"LnL?"

Roger smiled. "Limp, 'n Limber." I rolled my eyes. "Figures."

"I'll tell you all about it," Roger said, "because I want you to come to work for us."

"But I already have a job."

"This won't be full-time. It will only be when a

situation comes up where you can be useful."

"I don't know Sounds scary."

"BB, you are not particularly useful in scary situations. I wouldn't send you into anything much worse than what you've just gone through."

"What! This has been the most terrifying week of my life."

"Bullshit. After you've had a couple of days to rest, you'll start missing the excitement."

"Yeah, I don't think so."

"Just watch. It gets into your blood. Plus, it pays pretty well."

That stopped me. A few extra sheckles never hurt. "I'll think about it."

"Good. We'll talk soon." He slapped my knee and stood. "I've got to run. I have to talk to Nacho about what we want to do with Judge Hawthorne."

"What do you mean?"

"He's quietly arranged to change his name and move into an assisted living facility in Florida. Very private. Very hush hush. They'll probably never find out where he went or be able to investigate his questionable finances."

"So, what's to decide?"

"Whether we want to let him go or place a couple of well-timed anonymous calls before he can slip away." Roger winked at me and walked off.

Someone tapped me on the shoulder. I looked. It was Joshie, Nacho's Twink commander in training who had taken over running the volunteers on Monday. He looked good on Monday. He still looked good.

"Hi," I said. *Oh BB, you are such a silver-tongued devil.*

He smiled. It was a very nice smile. "I thought I'd say congrats on winning."

"Thanks. It was really good of you to step in. It helped."

He smiled again. It really was a nice smile. "Just doing my job."

I so wanted to keep him close for a bit longer. "Um

. . . I guess I also can thank you for saving my life. If you hadn't called the cavalry—"

"Well, I couldn't let you sneak off and die without saying goodbye."

"I must think of a way to show my appreciation."

Joshie wiggled his eyebrows. "Hmm. That sounds enticing, but I'm supposed to be heading out."

"Should I ask where?"

He shook his head and smiled again. He could smile at me all night and that would be fine. "If I told you, I'd have to kill you."

I raised an eyebrow. "And how would you do that?"

"Carnally. Long, luxuriously, and carnally."

This was going just where I dreamed it would. "When are you leaving?"

"I *was* going to leave tonight."

"Magawatta is very pretty in the morning light," I suggested and held my breath.

Joshie winked and nodded. "I think I'd like to see that."

I stood and handed Slasher over to Deb. "I'm outta here," I said.

Deb looked at me, then noticed Joshie. She smiled. "Have fun, big boy."

"I'll do my best," I said as I put my arm around Joshie. We headed to the door and into what I hoped would be a beautiful friendship.

The End

Also available from Any Summer Sunday Books

Any Summer Sunday at Nacho Mama's Patio Café
Adult Fiction
How far should you go to rescue a friend from her own desires?

Ghost Girl | A Mystery
Middle Grade Fiction
Sometimes a ghost needs a hand. Sometimes a guy needs a friend.

All books are available in print, audio and ebook.

Contact us for book club discussion questions and lesson plans. Class sets available.

Steve is available for presentations and Q & A sessions via online video platforms.

If you enjoyed our books, please post reviews online and share with your friends.

All books are available through our website, online retailers, and your local independent bookseller.

Visit us at:
https://www.AnySummerSunday.com
Steve@AnySummerSunday.com
Box 3306 Bloomington, IN 47402

CPSIA information can be obtained
at www.ICGtesting.com
Printed in the USA
LVHW100045061121
702558LV00001B/62